ROMANCE
& THE REAL ESTATE
SPY

Luci Hunt

authorHOUSE®

AuthorHouse™
1663 Liberty Drive
Bloomington, IN 47403
www.authorhouse.com
Phone: 1 (800) 839-8640

Published by AuthorHouse   09/28/2015

ISBN: 978-1-5049-3275-2 (sc)
ISBN: 978-1-5049-3276-9 (hc)
ISBN: 978-1-5049-3274-5 (e)

Library of Congress Control Number: 2015913670

Print information available on the last page.

This book is printed on acid-free paper.

Dedication

TO BILL: LOVE YOU FOREVER

Chapter 1

Caroline sat staring out the rain streaked window. Gloomy overcast days always made her think of the past and ponder the decisions she had made over the years. She went back over some of the circumstances in her mind and wondered if she had always made the right decisions when it came to men and her career.

The summer after graduation she met Bill Kincaid. It was one of the first changes to happen that would affect her life forever. It was not love at first sight like you always hear about, but it seemed the more dates they had the more she wanted to be with him all the time. He was the first man that seemed to have manners, believe in God, and actually had a job. They had just graduated from school and a lot of the boys were still looking for work but Bill was ambitious and his dad had heard about a job at one of the big companies in town. It didn't hurt that he was very handsome either. Bill was the kind of guy everyone loved. He didn't talk a lot but when he did he always had something to say that was interesting and you could tell he knew what he was talking about. Caroline and Bill were a perfect match since she was outgoing and he was shy. They found when they were together it was so hard to not be touching and kissing. It was like they were just meant to be together and they decided marriage would definitely have to be the next step. Caroline had always wanted to be a virgin when she finally got married so anytime they were alone it was more difficult to make sure she could keep that promise to herself.

Bill had called one day to say he had planned a picnic for that weekend. The weather had just started being warm enough that a trip to the park would be perfect. Caroline offered to pack a lunch and they made a time to meet. The park they went to had lots of beautiful trees and a large lake that was so clear you could see the bottom. They decided to lay a blanket on the ground next to the lake and enjoy their lunch. Bill seemed more quiet than usual. He turned to Caroline and kissed her passionately. Caroline was shocked since Bill was not usually so demonstrative in public. After the kiss he reached in his pocket and pulled out a box. He opened it and the most beautiful diamond ring she had ever seen was in the box. "Will you marry me? Every time I am with you I just can't help but want to show you how completely I want you, but I know how you feel about sex before marriage," he said. Caroline replied, "Yes, I want the same thing that you want. It is very hard for me to say no too," she whispered quietly.

They decided to get married as soon as plans could be made. It was going to be a small wedding since they didn't have a lot of money saved up. It wouldn't be as grand as Caroline had always thought her wedding would be but she spent all her available time trying to plan a wedding that would have memories that could stay in their minds forever. It was hard to plan a great wedding with very little money but wanting it to be nice Caroline tried to make it perfect.

Finding the perfect dress without spending a lot of her savings was proving to be hardest thing. Finally, after looking for a while, she found a friend who had cancelled her wedding and was never able to wear her dress. Her friend made her a great price and it fit like it was created for her. Everything seemed to be working out so great.

Unfortunately, a month before the planned wedding, nothing could have made things any worse than what happened next.

Chapter 2

One afternoon, about a week before the wedding, Bill called Carolyn to see if she would meet him that afternoon. She thought he sounded upset but she decided it was all the wedding plans. His job was getting harder since he had just gotten a promotion. They had not seen each other much and she was looking forward to the evening.

They decided to meet at their favorite place. It was a small comfortable restaurant that a friend of Carolyn's had opened earlier in the year. The décor was done so well with beautiful flowers placed just in the right places and the colors on the walls were bright and cheerful. Carolyn arrived first and ask for a table in the back. She wanted them to have privacy. Bill had sounded serious on the phone.

When Carolyn saw Bill walk in she knew it was something serious. As she watched him come closer she felt so proud to be marrying such a good looking guy. Every time she saw him her heart would swell up and she could hardly believe she had been lucky enough to find him. He was tall and muscular but even better than that he was good to her and everyone else he knew. Bill sat down across from her and proceeded to clear his throat. "Carolyn I have something to tell you and I don't exactly know how. When I went to the mailbox yesterday I found this letter there."

Carolyn could not imagine what the paper could say that was so bad. She proceeded to look at the paper still not knowing what it might be. It was bright yellow with some official looking writing on it. "What is it Bill?" she ask. Bill hesitated and then almost in tears he said, "My draft notice. I have to report for basic training two weeks from now." It took Carolyn some time to take in what Bill had just said. It was the 1960's but they hadn't even thought this could happen to them. None of their friends had been called up but so many of them had gone to college and Bill had started work right after high school. All she could think about was him

Being gone from her after they were finally going to be together forever. Bill had gone for his physical but that had been months ago and his eyesight was bad without glasses so we assumed he was out of danger of being called up.

"What now, said Carolyn?" Bill just gazed into her eyes and seemed speechless. You could tell he didn't know what to say next. "Are you sure you want to go ahead and be married?" he said. "Of course, why wouldn't I?" she said. He seemed relieved but it was hard to tell exactly why he had asked the question.

They both stayed and talked but Carolyn still could not find out why Bill was wondering if they should get married. They decided to go that evening to tell Bill's Mom and Dad. They were a very close family and they knew it would be an upsetting thing for them. His parents seemed to take it much better than they thought but his Mom was, of course, concerned about the death toll and Vietnam had one of the biggest. Bills sister had MS and he had been a big help at home doing a lot of the things his Mom couldn't do. It was really going to be a hardship on everyone for Bill to be gone.

Carolyn was still bothered by Bill's even questioning their wedding so she ask him over the next evening to see what she could find out. He seemed very quiet after she confronted him again but finally he told her. His friend had gone to Vietnam and it had changed him so much and Bill was concerned that it would do the same to him. He did not think it seemed fair to ask Carolyn to marry one man and have another come home. It was such short notice for everyone for them to cancel but he really wanted to wait at least until he got his permanent assignment. Carolyn said she would think it over that night and let him know something definite tomorrow.

It was a very long and sleepless night for Carolyn. She talked to her parents and a close girlfriend to get their opinions but she knew it probably was a good idea to wait at least until Bill knew where he would be spending the next couple of years. It was going to be hard because she had waited for marriage to finalize their love and now it was not going to happen.

The next day was filled with sunshine but not to Carolyn. She met Bill for lunch and let him know what she had decided. He seemed to be relieved but not happy either. They agreed to spend the next couple of weeks together every minute they could. They tried to do things where they would not be totally alone for long periods of time. It was too hard not to become carried away with their passionate feelings for each other. It seemed like there was not much to look forward to for a long time. There would be basic training, then advanced, and who knew from there. Almost everyone was going to Vietnam after training. Even the boys who had all gotten out the draft in the past were being sent. There would be no way of really knowing until Bill was out of advanced training where he would go. All they could do was hope and pray he would be assigned at stateside post.

Chapter 3

The decision had been made to cancel the wedding for now. Caroline wasn't so sure she wanted to wait for the honeymoon. She tossed and turned every night trying to decide what the right thing to do was. She loved Bill so much and the thought of having to wait to enjoy loving him with her heart, soul, and her body too, was unbearable. To her that was the ultimate gift to him so he could keep those thoughts close to his heart while he was gone. They were to meet that evening and she had made her decision.

Bill picked her up in his refurbished 442. He loved that car and would probably miss it as much as her but she hoped not. She always knew when he was outside her door because he revved the engine which she was sure the neighbors just loved. He was such a gentleman and came around to help her in the car. She slid across to sit right next to him as usual. Touching him as much as she could was so important. Who knew when she would see him again? They drove to their favorite steak place. Carolyn had said she needed to talk to Bill about something very important. They ask for a secluded spot in the corner booth. Carolyn and Bill loved this place since it was low lighting and beautiful music.

Carolyn ordered a glass of wine to help her relax. She looked into Bills eyes and he knew this was something serious. "What if we have the honeymoon?" asked Carolyn. Bill was taken back since he was not expecting her to ever suggest that. "You mean before the wedding?"

She nodded and gave a small smile. They had been into some serious lovemaking but both had decided to wait to be married before consummating their relationship. He thought a minute and said, "If you are sure. I don't think I can wait any longer to love you totally." Carolyn hugged Bill and he could tell she was very happy with his decision. "Let's make it special by going somewhere out of town and staying somewhere we have always wanted to stay," Carolyn said. Bill said he knew just the place but he wanted surprise her. They made plans for that weekend since it was the last weekend before Bill was to leave.

Bill had still not told Carolyn where they were going but she knew they were headed toward Louisville. It was a pleasant two hour drive. They enjoyed just being together so much they didn't even have to talk too much. Carolyn was a little nervous. She had heard so many horror stories about the first time. Carolyn and her best friend Maggie talked about everything and she had said it was really painful. She also told her some things that might help make it better. They drove up to a beautiful downtown hotel and Carolyn couldn't believe Bill could afford this place. It was known for its high prices and wonderful food. Bill checked them in and carried their bags. They had packed very lightly since it was just for the weekend.

As they reached their room Bill started to pick Carolyn up but she stopped him. "Let's wait on that until the real honeymoon. Some things need to be saved for the wedding," Carolyn said. It was a beautiful room with a sitting room and a large bedroom. The bed looked like it could hold a harem of women. Carolyn went and sat on it and the bed was like a big marshmallow. She had never slept on anything this luxurious. She walked into the bath and it was the largest tub she had ever seen. The fixtures looked like real gold. There were all kinds of beautiful toiletries on the sink. Carolyn could not help but feel this was the perfect hotel suite to lose her virginity in.

Bill offered to order room service and Carolyn decided to soak in the tub so she could feel extra special for Bill. It took forever to run the water to fill such a big tub but it was well worth the wait. Carolyn soaked as long as she felt she should without seeming to leave Bill waiting too long. She had bought a beautiful white lacey teddy just for this occasion. She had been tanning for a few days since she had very pale skin and wanted to look her best in the white teddy. She decided to wear her strawberry blonde hair down since it just looked sexier that way. One glance in the mirror before opening the door and Carolyn was quite proud of how she looked. She never thought of herself as being pretty but she just had a glow that she had never seen before. Carolyn took a deep breath and entered the bedroom.

Bill was standing by the window enjoying the wonderful nighttime view. As she entered the room, he turned and his eyes were like big blue saucers. He gasp as if she had taken his breath away and walked toward her. He kissed her like he had never kissed her before. His mouth pressed hard against her lips. He put his tongue on her lips and slowly moved it so it opened her mouth so their tongues could meet with desire. His hands moved down her body and were so warm. He caressed her all over while he was kissing her. She felt the kiss all the way to her toes. They inched slowly towards the bed and fell onto its soft feathery covers. It was like they hadn't seen each other for months. Carolyn did not realize how much she could want something like this when for months she had thought it was something she could not have before marriage. Bill began to kiss her neck and then he started moving his kisses down her breast and drew her nipple into his mouth. Being as innocent as she was Carolyn was at first shy but then she found that she quivered all over and it didn't really seem unusual at all. Bill then began to run his hands all over her and she could tell he was getting aroused. She was a little afraid when she could feel through his clothes just how excited he could get. They both starting taking the others clothes off and when they were both completely naked it seemed so natural. Like they did this all the time. Bill said, "I'm sorry but I cannot wait another minute to make us one." Carolyn did not even hesitate to let him know she approved in fact was eager to get to that part too. As Bill slowly eased into her. It was mildly painful but she had expected that. After the small amount of pain she felt it seemed she could explode from within. As Bill moved back and forth she could tell any minute the fireworks would begin. "Oh, my God, why did we wait for this?" said Carolyn. Bill could not even answer he was too busy trying to make this last as long as he could. Just as he would not be able to wait any longer Carolyn began to lose herself in ecstasy. She was unaware but she was moaning and Bill knew he would meet her there in a wonderful end to a new experience. After their lovemaking they both were exhausted but very happy.

There was no time for food after all. Carolyn and Bill spend the next two days catching up on what they had been missing all this time. Carolyn knew it would more difficult knowing another thing that she would be missing and how wonderful only the memories would have to be.

Bill had to leave Monday morning and she kept trying to put that out of her mind. She knew it would be one of the worst days of her life. He hadn't even left yet, and her heart already longed for him.

Chapter 4

B ill had left this morning and Caroline was already crying her eyes out. What once were blue like the sea were now red and swollen. She knew it would be hard but this was going to be something she never had to deal with. Yes, she had lost grandparents and aunts but for someone she felt shared her hopes and dreams to be gone for so long was something she could not fathom being able to stand.

That morning when the bus picked Bill up the whole family had gone. They left for the court house and hugged until he had to board the bus. They promised to write as much as possible and call whenever he could. He would most likely be out in the field for maneuvers so there would be no convenient time for Bill to call her. Back in those days not many calls were allowed. You had a few phones and a line that was very long. Usually the guys were just too tired to stand in a long line after a day of running up hills and carrying loads of equipment. Caroline watched as all the young men boarded the bus. You could tell they were trying to be brave but their eyes showed a different story. Eyes were straight ahead and almost staring. She felt they knew if they looked back it would be hard for them and their families. It was sad to see so many guys who had just started making their lives with careers to be pulled away for a war no one really wanted. Caroline rode home with his parents trying hard to be brave for them but it was the first time Bill and she had been apart for anytime at all.

Caroline thought each day would get easier but since she was not working and living at home there was so much time to spend just thinking about how much she missed him. She wrote everyday knowing he would get them all at once but not caring since she at least felt closer by sharing her feelings. He wrote as often as he could but by the time he came in for the evening it was lights out and besides he probably wouldn't have had the energy anyway.

Caroline did have her best friend Maggie to spend some time with. Maggie was selling real estate and very successful at it. At lunch one day Maggie suggested Caroline go get her license so at least she would have something to occupy her mind while Bill was gone. It was just a sixteen week course and Maggie would help her if she had problems. It seemed like a good idea since Caroline was putting off her education after high school until Bill and her had gotten married and settled into a life together.

After checking into the cost and schedule, Caroline decided to give it a try. She would start at the local university and go two nights a week for sixteen weeks. They required several tests and then a State final to get your license. Maggie had assured Caroline that the broker she worked for would be more than glad to hire someone as smart and stylish as she was. It was something new and exciting and hopefully would fill some of that extra time that Caroline spent feeling sorry for herself.

Caroline had not been to college yet so it was very scary entering a big university and finding her way around. The class was much larger than she expected but looked forward to meeting new people. The school was just built and had that new smell. As she found a seat she noticed most of the class was older than her but that made her feel even more confident. Her teacher had been a popular Realtor so she knew that he had experience and knowledge to pass along to others. There was a lot of homework and things she never imagined she would have to learn. This job was going to involve a lot more than she expected but she looked forward to the challenge.

By week three Caroline knew she was going to like Real Estate. She met a lot of nice people and they all were anxious to start work. The year Caroline picked to start Real Estate could not have been better. There were not a lot of agents and the competition was not as bad as it would be eventually. Some of the people in class would meet after school really got to know each other. One of the students was actually someone Caroline had gone to school with so they would sit together in class. Nancy had been class President, cheerleader, and Prom Queen. She was not in Caroline's group of friends in school but now that they were out of school they seemed to have a lot in common. Nancy had married right after school and her husband was drafted right away too. It was great to have a friend who could share this traumatic time with. Whenever

Caroline would talk about Bill, Nancy would listen but she never seemed to agree or disagree when it came to her husband and his being in the military too. It was almost like she had something to say but did not say it.

Time went by fast while Caroline was busy, however, she still had trouble sleeping because she was constantly thinking about Bill. When he wrote to her he made it sound like he was okay but she could sense a lot of homesickness in his words. He was even better writing about his love for her. Bill was always a little shy so she knew it was easier being able to write what he felt. She had hoped he could come home after Basic Training, however, they sent him right away to Fort Polk, Louisiana. It was so far away and with money tight she just couldn't drive or fly there. Caroline knew it was really hard in Louisiana since it was the middle of summer and really hot to be training but that is why they sent them there. That swampy, muddy, nasty terrain was as much like Vietnam as you could get in the States. It made both of them positive that he would be going overseas his next orders. He even wrote one week to tell her he had gotten a fungus on his feet and actually was given some time out of the swamp to heal up. It sounded like he was so happy even for a little relief. Every time Caroline received a letter, she felt so guilty for all the things she had and that Bill was doing without. It was unbelievable what these soldiers went through for us even the ones who didn't have a choice.

Chapter 5

Autumn was already in the air. The leaves were starting to fall and Indiana always was such a beautiful place to enjoy this time of year. The summer had passed slowly but it was almost time for Bill to come home for his thirty day leave. He would be given his next assignment and then have thirty days to report to his new base of operation. Caroline's final test was in two weeks and then her state test that same weekend in Indianapolis. She was hoping to have her test behind her and take some time to be with Bill.

They had written each other as much as possible. Some of Bills letters were sugar coated and others were downright depressing. Sometimes his platoon was out in the fields for days without anything but bare necessities. His feet were constantly wet and snakes were hanging from the large oak trees laden with moss. It was very hot at Ft. Polk since Louisiana was humid and being at Ft. Polk was like spending time in a sauna. He was looking forward to Fall at home. He said the only thing that kept him going was being able to think about seeing her again and spending some time together. Caroline didn't know if it was because he was dreading what his new assignment might be or if he was just preoccupied with all the training but she noticed he was not writing as much as he did at first. It was scary not being able to talk about what might be bothering him. Had he decided this time away from her might have made him think twice about their marriage? All Caroline knew was that time could not go fast enough before he came home.

Caroline had decided to make a decision about who to work for after Bill had left again. Maggie insisted she meet her broker so Caroline went to the Real Estate office where Maggie worked. It was in a very nice eastside office. The broker was also the leasing agent for the building so he had the main floor office and it was very impressive. It was a fairly new building and was very well decorated. The broker was Earl Callie and he seemed really nice. He was an older man and very distinguished looking. You could tell he was very particular about his business and he gave an air of professionalism that was very noticeable. He had a great reputation in the community. She also met his brother James who was his office manager. She could tell James was not as serious about things as his brother. He was more happy go lucky and it seemed he would be great to work with. There were not a lot of companies selling real estate at that time because the market did not have the demand that it would have in the future. She was glad it was a small company since she felt she would learn more from an office where everyone knew each other. She also got to meet some of the other agents and the secretary. There were ladies that she knew from the social page that would not have to sell houses but liked to for the notoriety. Caroline had heard from

Maggie that real estate had several agents who were Doctor's wives and lawyers wives. They all seemed very welcoming to her and made her feel at home. Earl Callie showed her where there would be a desk for her if she should decide to come with their company. Caroline could hardly wait to start being a real estate agent. It was so exciting getting to meet lots of people and using her outgoing personality to make a name for herself. The biggest downfall was it was commission only but she had seen Maggie make a lot of money after a little time in the business so she felt confident that she could also do well. At the time Caroline was beginning her career, a million dollars in real estate was a lot of money for someone to sell. Of course, that would change as the market expanded and there were larger priced homes and more competition.

As the time drew nearer for Bill to come home Caroline tried to put all her time into studying for her tests. She felt confident but had heard stories of many people flunking the State and having to take it over. Caroline was hoping to get a little closer to Nancy on this weekend away. They had always enjoyed each other's company but Caroline felt there was something that Nancy wanted to confide in her but kept holding back. They had planned on sharing a room to save expenses and that would give Caroline the opportunity to talk to Nancy in a more private situation.

The weekend of the test was there before Caroline knew it. She had passed her school exam at the top of her class. It was hard being excited but she was also very nervous. This was her future and what she really wanted to do. What if she couldn't pass the test? Nancy picked her up on that Friday afternoon and they drove to Indy to spend the night and get some more studying in. When they reached the hotel it ended up being a lot nicer than Caroline had expected.

Nancy had made the arrangements so Caroline had no idea where they were staying. Nancy always seemed to have extra money but Caroline knew she had a wealthy family so she was not surprised. They unpacked and decided to head out to eat and then return to study. They went to a place Nancy had been before that was very nice and the music was wonderful. The food proved to be excellent too. It just so happened they ran into some other students that they went to school with and really enjoyed the evening. It was the first time Caroline had actually noticed Nancy having a great time. There were some very nice looking men in their class and she noticed Nancy was drinking a little too much and flirting a lot. It was confusing but what the heck they might as well enjoy themselves this weekend. Caroline knew she was not interested in anyone except Bill but she felt like Nancy was old enough to know what she was doing and maybe she was just friendlier than Caroline had seen at school.

When they returned to their room, Caroline wanted to get to bed early so she could have rest for the next days test. Nancy was a little intoxicated and wanted to talk so Caroline decided what the heck she wanted to get to know Nancy more anyway. They sat on the side of the bed and talked for a long time. Caroline decided this was the perfect time to ask Nancy why she never mentioned her husband. Nancy hesitated for awhile and finally spoke. "I really didn't want to talk about my husband, Joe, until you knew what destination Bill would have assigned to him." "What does that have to do with anything?", ask Caroline. "My husband was injured very severly in Vietnam and is still being treated for his problems. I did not want to scare you and make you worry anymore than you already are." said Nancy with tears in her eyes. Caroline sat stunned for a minute. "Oh, my gosh I feel so bad for you. I could have been there for you and helped." "No I should not have told you now but it is just so hard to be your friend and not talk about it", said Nancy. So many of Joes friends did not come back but Nancy thought she had better not tell Caroline anything about what happened or it would depress her even more.

They talked for quite awhile. Nancy described how badly her husband was injured and all the rehab he had to have. He was affected both mentally and physically. She told Caroline how much she missed the person she had married. It had been very lonesome for Nancy since her husband was in a military hospital in Missouri and she could only see him on weekends. His recuperation would be long and he would not get to come home for many months.

They both decided it was time to get some sleep for tomorrow. Caroline was afraid this news would disable her thinking mode for tomorrow. She told herself over and over not everyone that went to Vietnam was hurt or killed. She had to believe that Bill might not have to go to Vietnam or anywhere else that was dangerous but they would just have to deal with it if he did.

Getting up that morning was really hard since both had gotten very little sleep but they were determined to do well on this test. Caroline didn't know what to expect but the room they took the test in was gigantic and there were hundreds of people from the whole state taking the test. She was so determined to do well but as she started the test everything she learned didn't seem to be on the test. There were lots of math problems and that was not Caroline's best subject. It was a two hour test with only 2 breaks. She finally got through the first part and started the law part of the exam. It was so hard since they had not spent a lot of time in class on it but were supposed to read the pamphlet they were given. She had done that but this was the first test she had on state laws. Caroline noticed people laying down their pencils and shoving back their chairs. That upset Caroline since she was far from over. By the time she was finished, almost all the class was finished. She handed in her paper and since Nancy was already finished she met her back in the room. Nancy felt good about the test which made Caroline feel even worse. It really scared her how hard it had been and how important it was for her to do well. The bad thing was they would not know their grade until it was mailed to them and there was no telling how long it would take for that.

In another week Bill would be home and Caroline could only think of him and how excited she would be to see him. Since Nancy had told about her husband's injury, Caroline tried to put aside any thoughts of something like that happening to Bill. It had been so hard being away from him that she did not know how she had made it through this time. If it hadn't been for her having classes and studying to keep her busy she could not imagine what she would have done. Bill was going to call and let her know when his bus would arrive in town and she would pick him up. Bill had been saving up so they could stay in a hotel for a week and they could get to know each other again. Living with her parents made it hard for Caroline and Bill to have as much privacy as they really needed. Her parents were not crazy about Caroline having sex before marriage but they felt both of them loved each other and understood why they did not want to wait. Caroline made sure her hair was looking extra good and she had been dieting so she could look her best for Bill. She had bought the sexist nightgown she could find. It was very skimpy. It would not be easy being naked around Bill but she knew she would get used to the idea very quickly.

The week flew by and before she knew it Caroline was waiting closely by the phone to hear from Bill. Every time the phone rang she jumped hoping it was him and yet afraid what he would have to say when she did hear from him. It would not be what she expected.

Chapter 6

There was a song that was called "It's A Long Way Home" but Bill was not thinking about that while on his drive back to Indiana. All he wanted was to get away from the heat and swampland he had been in for the last 4 months. He wanted to surprise Caroline so he didn't even call to let her know he was coming. He rented the smallest most reasonable car he could and headed home. The car he rented was on the small side but it was almost new and he didn't have to stop for gas but once. He had made extra money while he was gone by doing chores for the officers off base on the days he had off. Bill wanted their time together to be extra special. All he could think about was being back in his hometown and seeing the love of his life. His training had drained him of all his senses except the feelings he felt when thinking of Caroline. He had to watch his speed because he was in such a hurry to get home.

It was quite a trip from Louisiana to Indiana but he was so glad just to be going back he didn't really care if he had to drive all night to see Caroline. He needed the time to think about how he was going to tell her about his new assignment and talk to her about an idea that he and some of his friends had been planning. He had a lot of friends but some were really what he called his buddies. They were out in the field so much you had to rely heavily on others.

Bill bought some flowers on the way at a little store where he stopped for gas. When he was almost to Caroline's house he called her Mom just so someone would know he was coming and to make sure she would be home. He was feeling so nervous it was like going on their first date. He carried the yellow daises up and rang the door bell. Caroline opened the door and almost fainted. She looked at Bill like he was a stranger. He had lost a lot of weight, his hair was blonde from all the sun in Louisiana, and he looked like a different guy but not in a bad way.

"Oh, my god", said Caroline. You are such a louse for not calling first." She fell into his arms and they kissed for a long time. She had forgotten how he made her feel. She was thrilled and excited all the way down to her toes. They both went into the kitchen and sat down at the table. "So tell me before I faint where you are going to be stationed?" said Caroline. Bill looked indecisive and then he said, "I would rather we wait until we can be alone at the hotel. There will be plenty of time to talk after we get to know each other all over again." Caroline found that strange but she decided maybe he was right. Whatever he had to say could wait and if it was terrible it would ruin their first evening together.

Bill had booked the same wonderful hotel in the city and the suite was beautiful. He was so anxious to get a shower and actually feel like a real person for a change. He did not want to wear a uniform the whole time he was going to be home. When Bill was done showering he came into the room with just his boxers on and Caroline was amazed at how Bill had changed. His body was so muscular and tan. She could feel her knees shaking and it was almost like she was alone with a stranger. They were so new to each other in an intimate way but he was beautiful and he wanted her.

Caroline changed into her new sexy nightgown and could hardly wait to have Bill see her. When she walked into the room he was the one that was speechless. Caroline had always been kind of shy and bashful but this outfit screamed come and get me real loud. They met at the end of the king size bed and it was like they were one the rest of the night. Bill had been under so much pressure during his training and now he could show Caroline how much he loved her. Caroline was afraid she wouldn't know what to do but her natural instincts took over and they made love until they both were exhausted. It was even better than the first time. She felt less inhibited and let herself become his totally. They always kidded that sex was like riding a bike once you do it you never forget. The good thing is this was much better than riding a bike.

They awoke the next morning thinking it was morning but instead it was already lunch time. Bill promised Caroline they would go out for a nice lunch and he would talk to her about some options that he had. Caroline was confused about him having options, that didn't seem normal for a soldier to have choices, especially now during the Vietnam War.

Bill took Caroline to one of the really elegant restaurants close to the hotel. They ask for a quiet corner booth knowing they had a lot to discuss. They ordered and then Bill took at deep breath and then he said, "My orders are for Vietnam. I know we expected that but it is still hard for me to realize I would have to leave you for a whole year." Caroline felt her heart drop but decided she shouldn't be surprised. "What will that mean for you and me? A whole year apart and these last few months have been hard I can't imagine what that will be like", said Caroline. Bill nodded like he understood and then he told her he had talked to some buddies and they had an alternative plan. "What could you possibly do besides follow orders?" Caroline said. Bill knew the next part of the conversation was going to be hard so he took another sip of his glass of wine. "There are a couple of my fellow soldiers that feel we are not ready to go fight a war that no one wants us to be in and we probably can't win anyway. We are thinking of going to Canada," Bill said in almost a whisper. Caroline was very confused by what Bill said. It took her a minute to remember from newspapers and TV that some of the troops were escaping to Canada to avoid Vietnam.

Tears filled Caroline's eyes and she responded with some sense of desperation in her voice. "Why do you think that would solve anything? You can never come back if you flee to Canada they have made that very clear." Bill looked at her worried that he had made a big mistake talking about this now and not later. "I don't want to die and I want to be with you", he said.

Caroline ask if they could go back to the room. She had lost her appetite. It would take some time to think about what Bill had said but Caroline felt nothing but confused. She didn't want Bill to go to Vietnam but she didn't want to live in Canada the rest of her life either. She loved him so much but she had dreamed of some day owning her own real estate company and raising her kids near their Grandparents. It made her feel that it showed another side of Bill. She knew he was all man but to run away like a coward confused her. He never seemed the type.

They returned to the room and Caroline could feel everything had changed. Caroline told Bill how she felt and that she knew he was afraid but to give up their lives without family and country seemed like a drastic answer. He talked about how he felt and that he was not trying to be a coward but they were refreshing troops everyday to replace those that were wounded or killed. He would miss her so much for a year but they would not have to give that up if she would move to Canada. It seemed to help talking back and forth about their feelings and Caroline made it very clear she was not going to Canada. She understood if he wanted to go, but she could not give up so much even though she loved him.

They spent the rest of the week catching up on things, seeing things to help take their minds off what was ahead, and getting to know each other much better. The week went by fast and they returned to spend the next few weeks at Caroline's moms. Her parents gave them as much privacy as they could so it wasn't too confining. Caroline talked to her parents and her friends to let them know what Bill had ask her to do and they agreed that even though they couldn't blame him they did not want to see her leave and live that far away forever.

The time flew by and it was time for Bill to make a decision and leave for where he had decided to go. Since Caroline would not go to Canada Bill decided to proceed to Vietnam. He was scared and a person would be insane not to be. Caroline couldn't imagine the things he would see and have to do. She would miss him so much.

The morning he boarded his plane for Vietnam everyone was there. Her parents and his parents to wish him luck and let him know they were all supporting him. Caroline could already feel the lonesomeness seep in as the plane took off. It was like he took a part of her with him. Her heart felt like it could almost burst with the feeling of what it would be like to not see him for a whole year. They had promised to write as often as they could but mail was very slow to the states from Vietnam. Caroline had even sent stationary with Bill since she knew he might not have that available. She even sprayed some of his favorite perfume that he bought for her on each envelope so when he sealed the envelope it would make him feel she was right there.

Caroline spent the next few days feeling sorry for herself and crying a lot. Nancy called to see how she was doing and she told her about Bill thinking about Canada. Nancy understood more than anyone why he even thought of that as an option. Now that her husband was having so many physical and emotional problems she wasn't sure he had even came back. She said it was like he left the Joe she loved in Vietnam. Nancy also understood Caroline's attitude and agreed Canada would be awful too.

Caroline decided as soon as she could get her results about her Real Estate test she would get to work so she did not have time to think. It should be there any day and Maggie was really eager to see her come to work. Hopefully that would be a positive step for her life right now.

Nancy had received her test the first of the week so Caroline knew hers should be there soon. Nancy let her know she had done well and hoped the same for Caroline. Caroline received her results the next day and in addition a surprise along with it.

Chapter 7

J ust when Caroline thought she would never get her test results they were delivered. She slowly opened the envelope. This meant so much to her and the future she had planned. As she read the letter she was so excited she thought she would faint. It said she had passed. They did not tell you the score just fail or pass. She would have loved to know how she did but all she cared about was that she had passed.

Nancy was the first person she called since they had gotten so close lately. Nancy was excited for her and relieved that now she could also decide where to work. Nancy was not sure she wanted to work for such a small company as Maggie worked for. She had dreams of starting at a large company and learning from the best in town.

Later that afternoon Caroline received a call that shocked her. The owner of Dawson Realty called her and ask if she would meet with him tomorrow afternoon around 2 o'clock. Caroline was very confused and she ask Mr. Dawson why he was calling. He mentioned he had heard she had passed her Real Estate test and just wanted to see if he could offer her a job with the biggest and best company in town. It was amazing that she had just found out about the test and Mr. Dawson knew about it almost as soon as she did. She decided to go ahead and make the appointment. What could it hurt? It was probably a good idea to look at more than one company even though Caroline knew Maggie would be upset by her even talking to them. She had not made any promises so she felt she had to look at for herself no matter how good a friend Maggie was.

Dawson Realty had a great reputation. They did not hire just everyone that wanted to work there. She was very nervous but decided she did not want to be sorry someday about her choices. The owner of Dawson Realty was older and she had heard he was very stern and particular of just how things were to be done. The company had been in business for many years and had a lot of top producers in the city.

The morning of the appointment, Caroline went through her closet trying to find just the right suit to wear. She wanted to look professional and attractive since that was one of the things she noticed about a lot of the successful agents in town. She fixed her hair just right and even decided to wear glasses instead of contacts just to make her look smarter or least that's what she thought. Finding the office was easy since they were located in the downtown area and owned the biggest building in the area. When Caroline entered the lobby of Dawson Realty she was taken aback by the elegance but yet business like decorating. She told the secretary at the front desk who she was and that she was to see Mr. Dawson. The secretary said to have a seat and he would be right with her. It seemed like forever but really it was not that long before she was shown into a large office with windows overlooking the whole city. She noticed Mr. Dawson had his back to her when she entered. He said he would be right with her. He turned around in just a few minutes and she was astounded how young he was. She had heard he was in his 70's. She knew men looked younger than women of 70 but this man looked in his 30's.

"Sorry to keep you waiting Ms. Phillips but my dad had some important business and ask me to interview you today." "I am Derek Dawson". "No that's fine", she said. She wanted to say that this was their idea not hers but she would never have been so unprofessional. She knew this was going to be more nerve wrecking than she thought. Having an older man interview her would make her more comfortable than someone closer to her own age. Besides being young he was drop dead gorgeous. Caroline had not seen a man quite so handsome. He had blonde wavy hair that was styled just right. She could not help but notice he had big blue eyes and long eye lashes. He was wearing a white shirt that was without a wrinkle and a tie that matched the blue of his eyes just perfect. Caroline had to remind herself that she was here for an interview not a staring contest.

"Ms. Phillips or can I call you Caroline?" You are welcome to call me Derek" he said. "Yes please do, I would feel not as nervous if you do that." she said. "Oh, please don't be nervous. I just wanted to talk to you a little bit and see what your plans are now that you have passed your state test. We always like to interview the people who do really well on their exams," he said with a smile. She took a minute to think about that statement and ask, "How do you know my scores if I wasn't even informed of them?" "We have someone who works for the state who is allowed to release test results to us. They would

Chapter 8

It was a great day for Caroline's appointment. The sun was out and she felt like it was going to be a great day. Before Caroline had made her decision about possibly accepting the job, Mr. Dawson's secretary requested Caroline come in the very next day and early. Usually mornings were not Caroline's favorite time of the day but she was so excited she could not have slept that night anyway. Getting ready for the appointment was very hard to do. Her wardrobe was pretty scarce as far as really nice things were concerned and she wanted to look her best for Mr. Dawson. Finally she settled on a pink suit that she always had gotten compliments on. Caroline took extra time on her hair and makeup. Looking in the mirror she saw looking back at her a fairly attractive woman with a confidence she did not remember having for a long time. She had not made any promises about coming to work at Dawson Realty but she could not think of one reason not to. It's very possible they had decided she wouldn't be right for the job. Would they want an appointment just to tell her they didn't want her? She was so nervous during the first interview but mostly because Derek was so handsome and it was hard for her to concentrate on her words.

Traffic was extremely heavy this morning and Caroline hated driving downtown especially at Nine O'clock in the morning. She found a place to park her early model car and headed in the office. As she locked the car doors she thought to herself, "I sure hope I can afford a better car after I get a job." Her parents had given her this 1964 Chevy when she graduated school. It was not new then and it had not aged well from sitting out in the Indiana climate for several winters.

Riding up the elevator, Caroline noticed how many different offices were in the Dawson building. There was a lender, a title company, a surveyor, and everything else a Realtor would need all in one building. The Management offices were on the top floor and as she rode up the elevator Caroline double checked herself in the shiny stainless walls. When she reached the main office the secretary had her sit while she let Mr. Dawson know she was there. It was awhile before senior Mr. Dawson ask her to come in. She hoped she did not show her disappointment at not seeing Derek but she tried real hard to act like she was glad to see the elder Mr. Dawson.

Mr. Dawson senior was also an extremely handsome man even though he was older he was still very distinguished and well dressed. He apologized for Derek not being there but he had to go out of town for some business to attend to. Mr. Dawson proceeded to try to make Caroline comfortable with small chit chat but then he surprised her with his next sentence. "How would you like to train to be a quality control person for our firm? You are probably wondering what that is since very few, if any, Real Estate companies have one. Your job would be, once you are trained, to travel to our different offices and work as an agent just like everyone else. No one else would know what your true job is. We need someone to work with, even our experienced agents, and let us know if they are being professional by truly doing their job as top of the scale as we expect."

Caroline was stunned. She had never heard of such a job but there were a lot of things about Real Estate she was learning every day. "You mentioned training, sir. What kind of time would it take and how long?" Caroline asked. "I knew that would be something you would want to know right away so I have given you a written outline of your job and the pay. I will tell you a lot of people would love to have this job so early in their career. One of the reasons we decided this would be good for you is that you are not tied down with family, you can travel, and you have a very professional look and know how to carry yourself. Derek will be training you in our Indianapolis office. He will teach you the regular real estate business plus what to look for that would make an agent a person to report to us about," said Mr. Dawson. Caroline read over the outline and was amazed at the pay but she was concerned about the travel and how much she would be away once Bill returned home. She wanted to say yes immediately since it would give her an opportunity to work with the most experienced and smart agents in the State and it wouldn't be bad spending time with Derek. Oh, gosh, she thought to herself, I have been alone too long to even think such a thing is horrible.

Caroline told Mr. Dawson that she would love to think about the job and read the outline thoroughly so she could be sure it she could do the job one hundred percent. He told her he would give her a couple of days to think about it and if she had questions that weren't on the outline to call and he or Derek would try to answer any thing she needed to know. She was relieved he was giving her some more time to give her answer. It was something that would change all her plans but maybe in a good way. Caroline hated she couldn't just pick up the phone and call Bill because her decision could affect him too. She had not heard very much from him but knew it was because being out in the field, it was hard to find time to write.

Meantime thousands of miles away Bill was sitting in his tent at base camp finally getting a chance to read his letters from Caroline and being able to write back. He had been out in the field for two weeks. It was the rainy season, so getting to dry out and have feet that weren't soaking wet for a change was wonderful. Bill had been thinking many times the last month or so that he would give anything to have gone to Canada instead. Every day was another day to play hide and seek with the enemy and he was really tired of getting shot at. Caroline had mentioned a job she was considering but promised to write more when she knew for sure. Caroline's letters sounded like she was adjusting to life without him by keeping busy. She had said she might be working for another agency since she had done so well on her test. He knew she would do great. She was so bright and her future was going to be a great one he just wasn't sure he could be in it. He wanted to be but Bill could already feel changes in himself from being in the field and seeing so many of his friends die. There is no way anyone could have told him it would be like this. It was still many months until time to ship home and time just went by so slowly. He wrote Caroline a letter and told how much he loved her and missed her. He never told her the horrors he was going through since that would just make it hard on her too and she couldn't do anything about it anyway.

Two days later, Caroline had decided to take the job. If she did not have to travel too much in the future she could do it. She called and told Senior Mr. Dawson that she would love to work for him. He explained to her she would need to travel to Indianapolis and be gone only a week for training. They used their main office in Indianapolis for training everyone from the new to the experienced. Mr. Dawson told her that Derek would be going along so he could spend time explaining to her what the other part of the job involved. He assured her the purpose of her job was perfectly ethical and it would be a wonderful way for her to learn everything to make her an excellent agent. Caroline could hardly wait to get started. She was scheduled to leave the first of next week and was anxious to get out and buy some new clothes to make her wardrobe one that would give her extra confidence since they already seemed to be so sure she would be great at this job. Caroline found herself worried about being on a plane with Derek and being able to find something to talk about because she knew she would be a nervous wreck.

While she had time, she decided to write Bill and let him know what she would be doing and hoped he would be okay with her doing something a little different than originally planned. When she talked to her other friends she did not go into the part about her job being more than just an agent. She was afraid it might hurt her chances at being good at watching first hand how the agents at Dawson Realty were doing business. She almost felt like she was signing up for the Realtor CIA. She could not imagine what she could possibly discover by getting close to other agents but apparently both Mr. Dawson's were evidently suspicious of it happening or were aware of someone in particular who might be not exactly the agent they wanted working for them. Caroline was excited just about learning from different people how to sell real estate. She knew being a new agent it could take years to learn anywhere else.

As the time grew nearer to go to Indianapolis Caroline was so excited but also afraid of failing. She borrowed some money from her parents and bought some things nicer than she usually wore. This was going to be special and she wanted to fit in with all the other people she would be working with. The company was paying all her expenses for staying in Indianapolis so it seemed it might be a nice way to get away from the same old days of worrying about Bill and seeing on the news the casualties that were happening every day. Caroline had lunch with Nancy to let her know what she had decided about going with a different company and also to see how Nancy's husband was doing. They had a wonderful lunch and Nancy ask if maybe she could join Dawson Realty once Caroline had spent some time getting to know the routine and how it was going to work out. Of course, she never mentioned the purpose of her job to Nancy. Caroline invited Maggie to meet with her before she left. She felt bad letting Maggie down since it was her idea for Caroline to even try real estate. When Maggie found out where Caroline was going to be working she looked awed. "I have tried to get on there forever. It is really hard to get hired and I hear the money is terrific. I am so happy for you and keep in touch so we can do business together."

Caroline tossed and turned the night before she was supposed to be at the local airport to meet Derek. She got up early so she would have plenty of time to get ready. She had already packed two days earlier just to be sure she didn't forget anything. Caroline asks her Dad to drive her to the airport so she did not have to leave her car for a week. On the way to the airport it was pretty quiet. This was one of the first times Caroline had been away without her parents for any length of time and she knew they were worried. She tried to put her Dad at ease by letting him know how excited she was and what a great adventure this would be. As she arrived at the airport Caroline looked everywhere for Derek so she would know what gate and where they were sitting. He had the tickets so she was very nervous. She was always early though so she tried not to get to upset. Waiting she sat looking over the runaway inside the glass enclosure. For a small airport theirs was really done well. You could watch take offs and arrivals from the waiting area. She had her mind on wondering which plane was theirs and looking at her watch when Derek sat down next to her. She did not even have to look to see who it was. His aftershave was one of her favorites and she remembered how he had worn it at the interview. It was going to be a long plane ride. Not really but she couldn't imagine sitting next to this man for 2 hours and know what to talk about.

Chapter 9

Boarding the plane Caroline kept thinking about the fact she had only flown once and she did not particularly like it. Somehow having Derek with her made it seem okay and not scary. She noticed as they walked together to their seats how all the other women were watching him. He wore a suit that was tailored to fit him just perfectly and every hair was in place. His tie matched his shirt perfectly and there is not one woman that did not look. When they reached their assigned seats Derek cordially let her go first and said, "If you want the window seat that is fine with me. I have so much work to do I won't get to enjoy it anyway."

The plane left the airport right on time and took off smoothly to their destination. Caroline tried not to talk a lot to Derek since he had so much work to do, however, she could not contain herself from asking what their schedule for the rest of the week would be. Derek began to explain what he expected of her. "We will start the week by going over all the State forms you will have to become accustomed to filling out, some of the rules of the company, and time to meet agents at our Indianapolis office," he said unlike he was upset with her for bothering him. "When we finish those things I will go over what your job will be and how we will go about having you help us discover any inefficiency in the agents we have working for us," he added. In her need to not seem nervous she said, "I can hardly wait."

Indianapolis was only about a two hour trip so Caroline read a book she had started and Derek began working on his computer. Time went by really fast and they were there before she had even gotten two chapters done. They caught a cab to the hotel. The hotel was adjoining the real estate office making it so convenient for going to and from classes. It was a beautiful building and stood out against the skyline of the Indiana capitol. When they entered the hotel everyone knew Derek, of course, so they received star treatment. As she was shown to her room by the bell boy she was awe struck by the beauty of the carpeting, light fixtures, and paintings on the wall. It was the nicest hotel she had ever seen much less stayed in. Derek was joining her later since he had business to attend to in the office building next door. He told her tonight she could just relax and they could go to dinner if she liked. If only he knew how ridiculous a question that seemed to her of course she would rather do nothing else. Caroline would have been very disappointed if her first night in a strange town she would have to forage on her own for dinner. She entered her room not knowing what to expect. It wasn't really a hotel room. It was more a suite with a bedroom, living room, bar, and bath. There were beautiful flowers as she entered and you could smell the scent all over the room. She read the card and it was from the real estate office welcoming to their Indianapolis office and joining their company. Caroline had not received flowers very often and least of all ones this beautiful.

After Caroline hung up her clothes and was settled in, she decided to soak in the big tub that was in the beautiful bathroom. Sitting on the sink were all kinds of spa soaps and bath salts. She felt like a queen. When the bath was as warm as she could stand it she slid in and felt like she could stay in the tub for days. Every muscle in her body relaxed and she almost fell asleep.

When her bath was done, Caroline slipped on one of the beautiful robes provided by the hotel and decided to make sure her every inch of her looked good for dinner that night. As she was almost done the phone rang. "Can I pick you up in about an hour," said Derek. He had caught her off guard since she was thinking that people ate later in big cities but she didn't really care she could be ready anytime for seeing what there was to see in Indianapolis. "Yes, I will be ready by then. Do you want me to meet you downstairs?" said Caroline. "No I am in the room just next door so I will come by and walk down with you and then we will take the company car to eat. I am thinking about taking you to the greatest steak place you probably have ever been. Is that okay?" Derek said. Thinking about him being just next door, made Caroline hesitate because her mind was going in a million different directions. After what seemed a long time but probably wasn't, Caroline said that would be fine she would love a great steak.

It was very exciting to be going somewhere special and getting to know your boss right away. She was very careful what she wore and decided to dress informal but not casual. Caroline had experimented with putting her hair up for her bath and it looked so good she just left it that way. Trying to look her best she took more time with her makeup than usual and as she looked back at herself she felt confident that she looked as good as she had ever looked. Of course, her face was flushed from being so excited and taking that wonderful warm bath. Before Caroline knew it Derek was at the door. When she opened the door, there stood Derek in a polo shirt and jeans. She was so glad she had not dressed too formally. He looked as good in casual clothes as a suit. Everything matched and was in place as usual. It took him a minute to come in and she hoped it was because he appreciated how she looked and would proud to take her anywhere. After he came, she ask if he wanted anything to drink. "No," he told her. "I don't drink except a little wine with meals." As he held the door for her she was so close to him that she could feel his breath on her neck. It sent chills up her body but she tried to act like nothing was wrong.

The steak place he took her was nothing fancy but it was crowded so she knew it was probably a regular place for locals. They ordered their supper. Caroline was almost too nervous to eat but thought it would be rude not to order steak since that's what they came out for. As they sat waiting for their meal Derek started the conversation with a personal question. "Are you seeing anyone seriously? I know you didn't want a lot of out of town work so I assume you probably are." Caroline didn't really mind the question since she did want the company to know exactly what her future plans might be. "Yes, my fiancé and I were planning on marriage, however, he was drafted and now is in Vietnam," she told him. Derek looked somewhat disappointed but maybe she was just hoping that. "I just hate that war. It is so hard on everyone especially the men who have to go and leave behind their family. I was lucky and due to the fact I was attending college for 4 years I was able to be exempt from being drafted," he said. About that time their food arrived and she had wanted so bad to ask him if he was seeing anyone but it was probably too blunt a question coming from an employee so new with the firm.

They enjoyed their meal without talking much. The food was so good Caroline actually ate more than usual. She had some wine with her meal which was not like her but she wanted to have help relaxing and thought that would do it. After her first glass she had another and at that point she was feeling really good. She wanted the evening to last forever. Since it was getting late they decided to go back to the hotel so they could get an early start tomorrow and she wanted to have plenty of rest in order for her to be ready to learn everything she could about real estate.

The next morning Caroline called home to be sure everything was okay and to let them know she was looking forward to the week ahead. Her Mom and Dad had been very supportive of her entering such an uncertain job market. Caroline's mother told her there were some letters from Bill. Caroline told her Mom she would write him something that night so he wouldn't be worried if she did not answer for a week. As soon as she hung up she wrote a letter to Bill explaining what she was doing and that she would write again when she arrived home.

Bill was glad to finally receive a letter from Caroline. He knew she was busy with the new job but he still loved getting letters from home. It was evident that she seemed to be enjoying the learning process, however, he was a little jealous of her working with a man a little older than they were and from the way she talked very attentive. It had been hell out in the jungle every few days. It was the monsoon season and trying to keep your feet dry was impossible and it was hard to tell your enemy from the soldiers fighting on the side of the United States. He had made some friends but was afraid to get too close to them since they might be killed before he went home. It was awful having to shoot at people and kill them. He had been raised in church and taught "Thou Shall Not Kill" and now it was kill or be killed. The more he thought about it he wished he had gone to Canada. Maybe Caroline would have changed her mind and gone with him.

Caroline had breakfast at the hotel coffee shop and headed to the Real Estate office next door. The Indianapolis office was even more beautiful than she could imagine. You could tell they were a very successful office just by walking into the entrance. The girl at the front desk seemed to be expecting her and showed her to a small conference room with computers at individual desks. She seemed to be the first one there so she found a desk close to the front and waited for some of the other agents. She had forgot to ask how many other people would be training with her assuming it would be quite a few since it was such a big company. As time went by and Derek arrived she began to feel she was going to be the only one in the class. Am I really early since no one else is here?" Derek looked up from putting his papers in order and said, "No, I decided that we would work better just the two of us. That way I could explain what your other job will be without a lot of people being curious." "Oh, okay," Caroline said with some trepidation in her voice.

They proceeded to spend the day by going over filling out the offer to purchase, listing agreement, and any other necessary forms to sell real estate. They took time out for lunch in the hotel and then proceeded to cover the rules and regulations of the company and Multi-List system. It was a lot to comprehend at once but Derek assured her that she would not be expected to be able to fill them all out at once. The longer she filled them out the easier they would get. He let her know she would not be left on her own until she felt comfortable in doing the job well.

The next few days went by fast since Caroline was so busy learning everything she could. It was nice getting the full attention of the Derek since he made it all seem so easy. After some time she felt like they had known each other forever. It would really be a joy working for someone you liked so much.

On the last day he went over what her other job would be. He explained he had a feeling that some agents were not performing ethically but could not be sure. "I will not tell you who to suspect. It is normal for new agents to shadow experienced agents so no one will mind you tagging along. I will assign you to someone new every couple of weeks. You will not only get to practice what I have taught you but also see firsthand how these agents do business. I feel I do not need to point out what could be wrong it will be something probably that anyone could see as not being profession or ethical. You can start next week with one of the agents we have had for years. She is a top producer and I know you will have a lot to learn from her."

Caroline was anxious to get back home and catch up with Bill's letters. She felt guilty enjoying her time away and not thinking about him every second like she did before she took this job and started training. The flight home was uneventful. Derek seemed to have more time to talk and she enjoyed learning more about him personally. Apparently he had been engaged for awhile but it did not work out. He wasn't dating much since he was always so busy. It was terrible of her but she thought to herself some girl will really get a catch someday. Once she was home again she would get busy with business and not being with Derek every day.

That Monday she was supposed to meet Patricia the agent Derek had talked about. She recognized the name from signs and billboards around town. It was a little scary thinking about learning from an expert and spying on her also. Caroline was excited to start learning the business and start making some real money not just a small weekly salary.

Chapter 10

Monday morning came sooner than Caroline had hoped. She dreaded the meeting with Patricia but she knew it was going to be something she would have to get used to. It was so scary learning from one of the best in the business. It was like starting at the top but she should be thankful for the trust that Derek had for her ability to follow through. Caroline had heard that Patricia was a tough cookie and expected a lot from everyone including her customers but apparently it had gotten her where she was. Caroline carefully picked out one of her nicest outfits so Patricia would think she deserved to be her assistant and looked in the mirror. Caroline felt she looked okay. Without someone to tell her all the time how she looked, like Bill used to do, it was hard to have much self confidence. She had let her hair grow longer and highlighted so it would make her dirty blonde natural hair look so much better.

As much as Caroline dreaded the meeting that Monday Patricia did too. She was used to doing things her way and whenever it was convenient. Patricia had been in real estate long enough to work smart not hard. She had found if you listened to your clients and could figure out what they were thinking you could narrow down what they wanted even if they didn't know themselves exactly kind of house they were looking for. Having a newbie follow her around for two weeks was not going to be fun. Some things you just want to keep to yourself when you are tops in sales and want to keep it that way. She figured this new one would not last anyway. They hardly ever did. For some reason Derek had seemed to be interested in her learning from someone who he knew would teach her how to do it right. The company had promised Patricia extra commission if she would spend time teaching her some of her sales techniques. Of course, she would keep some of her secrets to herself and she would never disclose her client list. It was too hard to gain people's confidence and their coming back time after time was what made a successful Realtor.

Caroline arrived at the office early so she could get her mind around what her job would be. She rearranged her desk over and over until she felt she was being fanatical. Around 10 o'clock Patricia came in and stood in front of Caroline's desk. She cleared her throat to get Caroline's attention, "I'm sorry I am late, Mondays are just crazy after a long weekend of working. If you would follow me to my office I will show you how I keep everything in order and we can talk about what we will do for the next two weeks." Caroline looked up startled, "Yes, I am ready when you are."

They walked down a long hallway to Patricia's office. It was very secluded and as they entered Caroline could not believe what a beautiful office it was. This office was nicer than Derek's. It had windows looking out over the city and even its own private bathroom. There was a beautiful carved bookcase that was full of books lining one whole wall. Patricia laid her things down and proceeded to sit at her desk. She said quite abruptly, "I will let you accompany me to any new listings or showings but I will do my present work on my own. It expected that you will just be observing and you will need to bring a pad and pen to every appointment. I want you to learn to do some of the things such as measuring and taking pictures not just the interview end of the appointment." Caroline was taken back a little by Patricia's demanding voice but she answered quite nicely by saying, "Anything I can do to learn this business." Patricia was seemed kind of surprised how nice Caroline had answered as she usually had people not react well to her bossiness. "Let me get my things together we have an appointment at 11 to list a property," Patricia said. That day went pretty smoothly. Caroline ended up being more of a servant than an assistant but she did her best to just listen and learn. Patricia was very professional and knowledgeable to the client. Caroline could see how she was so successful.

Patricia was real surprised the new agent was attractive and smart too. She had very good manners and seemed to learn quickly. She could see now way Derek seemed to want her to succeed. It was hard to get young people into the business since it was commission only. They came in and out like the office door was a revolving one. She understood how hard it was to get started it had not been easy for her.

Patricia had started working as an assistant for another agent just to learn the ropes when she began 10 years ago. It had been difficult needing to earn lots of money right away and finding without the social contacts it was practically impossible to succeed. She had gotten lucky and learned a lot from the agent she worked for. Unfortunately, that agent became ill and passed away suddenly. It was really hard losing someone who had become a good friend. The company gave Patricia all her leads and since she had worked with a lot of them anyway by screening calls and making appointments for the other agent it was a blessing for Patricia.

The two weeks flew by and at the end of the time Caroline was to leave Patricia and move on to another agent Patricia let her show a house to a prospective customer on her own. It was kind of scary but also exciting. They were to be picked up that evening and knew exactly what house they wanted to see. Caroline noticed it was a listing with her own company so she would make even more if these people made an offer. She picked them up at their house and they seemed really excited to see the house. They had driven by and just loved it. Caroline could see why. It was an absolutely beautiful French Country home and was in an excellent neighborhood and well taken care of. As was normal Caroline had called ahead to see if it was convenient to show the house and it ended up being vacant which was even better. They entered the foyer and it was just as beautiful inside as outside. They removed their shoes and their feet sunk down like walking on a cloud. As they moved from room to room it appeared the whole house was decorated well. Custom drapes, crown molding, and a kitchen to die for. The buyers seemed excited and started placing furniture. That was one of the signs Patricia had told her was good. That meant they were serious. There was a spa room on the data sheet that she noticed but it did not detail what was in that spa room. It could be a sauna, hot tub, or just about anything you could imagine. It was the last room they looked at since it was in the back of the house. Caroline was as excited as the buyers to see what was in the room. She opened the door and much to everyone's delight it was not a disappointment. It had a sauna, work out equipment and walking further into the room there was a hot tub in the corner. At that moment time stood still, there in the hot tub were two totally naked occupants in a very compromising position. Apparently they were not even aware anyone was in the house much less looking at them. The client screamed when she saw them and Caroline immediately backed her clients out of the room as quickly as she could. The female buyer was very red faced and the gentleman buyer looked like he had never seen a naked women. Caroline ask them to proceed out back and look at the yard and she would see why those people were there and get them to leave immediately. Reentering the room Caroline was both mad and embarrassed. It seems the listing agent, Emma, had been given permission to use the hot tub anytime she wanted. "I thought it would be okay this late to be here. I didn't realize you were showing the house. I am sorry," Emma said as she proceeded to grab a towel and her clothes. Caroline did not recognize her male friend but he was more horrified than Emma. Caroline tried to control herself and said, "Is this something I can expect all the time? I wasn't told anything about this kind of thing when I was in training." By the time Caroline finished her sentence they had both gone out the door and into the garage. Apparently that is why she didn't notice a car at the house and was not expecting someone else to be there. Caroline proceeded to find the buyers and make sure they were okay. They didn't seem to be as upset as she thought they would be and they were excited about how nice the backyard was. After getting back in the car, Caroline ask them if they were interested enough to make an offer. "We would like to talk to our banker in the morning. If you would call back around noon tomorrow we will give you an answer. It is everything we want if the finances will work out," the buyer said. Caroline was so relieved she could hardly contain herself. She thanked them and went back to the office. Immediately Patricia ask her how things went but she only disclosed they were very interested and she needed to contact them at noon tomorrow. "I would not have let them get away that easy. It is easier to have them write the offer and worry about the financing later," Patricia said in a haughty sort of way. Caroline could only remember what happened and knowing Patricia she probably would have gotten Emma fired if it had been her showing.

It had been a very stressful day so when some of the office was going out after work she decided she could use a drink and with no one to rush home to she decided what the heck. There were about 10 or so of them going. As they jumped into a couple of cars, Caroline ended up in Derek's. She was in the back seat thank goodness. They were all discussing their day and laughing about things that happened so she just listened. A couple of times she looked in the rear view mirror to see Derek's expressions and he always seemed to be looking her way. At one point she quit looking just so it didn't seem obvious that she had been checking him out. She hated how she felt around him. It was like a feeling you get when something great happens to you. Goosebumps ran up and down her arms and legs. It was hard to pay attention to the conversation but she did her best. "Anything new with you today Caroline", Derek asked. Caroline had to ponder her answer for a minute. "I did get to show my first house by myself," she said. "And how did that go? "Did you get it sold?" one of the other agents ask. Caroline looked to the mirror to see if Derek was looking and answered almost too quickly, "Not yet. They seem very interested though." He seemed to smile as soon as she said that. Almost like he was really proud of what she had done.

When Caroline returned home she was glad to be able to relax. She had returned to find a letter from Bill that day wanting to know if she would join him in Australia for his R&R. The soldiers that were in Vietnam were offered the chance to take a week with family to relax and get away from the war. She didn't know how she would answer that question. The expense for going would have to be paid by her and right now she had just started being able to save a little. She really wanted to see Bill but it wasn't going to be easy leaving her job so soon to spend a week away. Caroline had done nothing but dream about that first time they made love and how great it felt to be loved like that. She almost regretted deciding to have sex before he left because it just made her miss being made love to and Bill. She would just have to think about what to do for awhile. They were not going for a month so she decided to write and let him know she was working on getting away and if she could get enough money together.

The weekend flew by and Caroline had not been able to decide anything yet about going to Australia and she knew she could not keep Bill waiting forever for an answer. When Caroline arrived at the office she decided to see if Derek was in and if he was busy. She ask his secretary if he was busy and she announced Caroline was there to see him. He immediately opened his door and she ask if she could have a minute of his time. "Sure I have most of this morning and afternoon. What do you need? I wanted to talk to you about how things went with Patricia anyway," he said. Caroline hesitated not knowing if it was appropriate to ask Derek to help make a personal decision but he had said anytime she needed help to ask him. "I need to know if it would be a problem in the near future if I would take a week off for to travel to see Bill. I just can't seem to justify spending money to fly to Australia and take time away just as I am getting started." Derek turned his back to her and seemed to thinking before he said, "I feel like if you want to see Bill you need to go. We can get you with the next agent for training and then you can have time off to go to Australia. I—we will miss you around here but you must see Bill I am sure he needs all the support he can get fighting that terrible war." Caroline noticed Derek had stumbled over his words and accidentally said he would miss her. It was like she was hoping he would say she couldn't go or something so she wouldn't have to be the one to make the final decision. She was really confused now.

Derek finally turned back around and said, so how did the two weeks with Patricia go? Was there anything out of the ordinary that happened?" Oh if he only knew but Caroline wasn't going to go there right now. "I learned so much from her. There were a few things she did but I don't think any of them would warrant a lot of concern. She tends to sway people to neighborhoods she thinks they should live in instead of letting them see everything in all areas and make that choice themselves. Also, she seemed excessive with a client who needed to back out of a purchase because he was ill and she demanded a letter from his Doctor," trying to sound positive about her experience.

He seemed surprised by those things but not too upset. "I will talk in staff meeting about steering customers and how it is against the law if they prove you were doing it because of prejudice. As far as the Doctor note I feel that was to protect the seller so even though it was harsh it probably was the right thing to do. It seems you did a good job. I have asked Patricia for a report back about your work and if she feels you will be a good agent just to make everything look like the ordinary training of an agent. I have an idea, let's talk more over lunch about this trip thing and maybe I can help you decide what to do," Derek said. Caroline seemed surprised by Derek caring so much but she told him sure after she caught up on phone calls and paperwork. They decided to meet at one of the restaurants close by. As Caroline left the room Derek said, "I want you to work with one of our other top producers the next two weeks. Have you met Emma?"

Caroline decided to walk to the restaurant so she could think more about what next week would be like. Working with the "naked" Realtor was going to be quite interesting. It was a beautiful day and she needed to get out and clear her head. Derek had reached the restaurant before and was sitting in the back booth. It was quiet back there. She was relieved since this restaurant always was busy during lunch. She slide into the seat opposite to Derek and noticed he had already ordered her iced tea. It was nice to be taken care of for a change. "Hope ice tea is okay. Thought that is what you drank but wasn't sure," he said. "Oh that's great. I hope I didn't keep you waiting. I returned my client calls and finished up some paperwork. The last call was terrific. The people I took to see the house on Oak last night are going to make an offer. It will be my first. I am so excited," Caroline couldn't help but brag. "That's wonderful. I knew you could do it. You seemed to give the impression something might make them not want it but I have seen that house and it is wonderful. I knew it wouldn't last. Have you made any decisions yet about going on your trip? I know you were having so much trouble," Derek said looking into her eyes. Caroline tried to avoid looking right at him. Those big blue eyes were like her mom used to refer to as bedroom eyes. "I still can't decide. It's hard to leave here right now," she said meaning that minute too. It felt so good to sit and have lunch and to be able to talk business and personal things. Derek was a really good listener. "I have a proposition for you. Don't take this wrong but I really have liking spending time with you and I would love for us to be able to see each other outside the office but I would never interfere with your present relationship. I do, however, have to believe sometimes you're feelings for Bill have changed. I would like to pay your way to Australia so you can see if those feelings are still there," he said sincerely. Caroline sat shocked for a minute then said, "Why would you want me to go if you think you want us to see each other?" Derek answered her right away, "I have the feeling sometimes your love for Bill might have grown cold because of his distance and your love of this job. I think if you go there you can see if you still love Bill as you did. He deserves to at least see you after all the time you have been apart. I feel a letter from you to say you are not going would be unfair to you and him." Caroline thought about what Derek just said. She let him know she would need to think about his offer. Not that she didn't agree with him but seemed crazy he wanted to pay for it. They finished their lunch and he walked back to work with her. Walking next to him was great. He was so handsome and now that she knew him better so nice too.

When the day ended and Caroline was home she decided to write a letter to Bill. If Derek was willing to pay for her to go it meant she really should. It would be a once in a lifetime trip. Australia was a beautiful place to go to with beautiful beaches and so many things the states didn't have. She would never let Derek pay her way. Something happened today that made her feel like her future was in this trip. She was so glad to have the decision about going off her mind. Now she could think about next week and wondered if Emma would be treating her different because of the spa room incident. Oh, God!

Chapter 11

Caroline had never been in the office after five p.m. but sleeping was not an option lately. She wanted to get all the paperwork finished that she had started with Patricia so she could start fresh with Emma. Everyone had gone home and it was so quiet it almost hurt her ears. It was nice in a way; however, she was used to the hustle and bustle of the large office and the excitement it brought to the job.

There were no cars in the parking lot when Caroline came in so she thought she was alone until she heard noises. It sounded like someone moving furniture around. She decided it must be the cleaning people and went on to do her paperwork. The amount of necessary forms was beyond what she had imagined but she had really caught on to everything really fast. Caroline was finding this time alone great for her being able to concentrate. No more worrying about going to Australia now that she was going and excitement of seeing Bill again and getting to see a beautiful country.

Another noise came from downstairs. It was starting to frighten her since it was strange and not like someone working late. It was more like things being moved around. Caroline decided to call Derek since he might know what the sound was. Maybe he had ordered some work done.

Derek answered the phone right away. "Yes, Caroline?" "Derek I am at the office late and I thought I was alone but there are some noises coming from downstairs. I am a little scared."

Derek sounded surprised she was still at the office. "I'm not too far away. I'll be right there. Sometimes we have mice wondering around downstairs but I want to be sure," he said. "I don't imagine mice would be making that much noise."

As soon as she hung up Caroline felt stupid. She really didn't mean for him to take his time out to worry about her. Well, it was nice to have someone concerned about her. She had been on her on for awhile now and it was a lonesome feeling.

Derek arrived in just a few minutes and said that he would check out downstairs. There had been offices down there at one time but agents complained it was too cold so they used it to store old desks and supplies. Not long after going downstairs Caroline could hear loud talking and Derek came back up looking shocked. "What was it?" Caroline said to him. He hesitated and then said Emma was down there and he didn't want to discuss it until later. "If you don't need me anymore I will be going unless you want me to walk you out," Derek replied. Caroline could not help but notice his flushed face and that he needed to leave right away. "No I still have work to do. If you feel it is safe to stay here I will. Thanks for the offer though," she answered.

Caroline probably should have gone home but she wanted to wait and see if Emma came back upstairs so she could see what happened. Since she had to work with her next week it would be nice to talk to her about what their schedule would be on Monday. Caroline finished her work and still no Emma. There was a back door so she assumed Emma had gone out that door and not passed her desk. Walking to the car was a little scary. It had gotten really dark by then and ever since the office incident she was a little on edge. Apparently, everything was okay. Maybe Emma was having trouble finding something and Derek was trying to help her.

Monday morning came too soon for Caroline. She had dreaded seeing Emma after the house fiasco but she had sold the house so Emma was now her best friend. That was how real estate was. If you sold something of another agents they immediately became your friend for life even if they had ignored you forever before that. The office was buzzing with Monday morning business left from the weekend. Caroline checked in at the front desk and ask if Emma was in yet. The secretary said she was in Derek's office but that she would let her know I had arrived. "Just tell her I am ready to get started when she is," Caroline said.

Emma was in Derek's office for a long time and came out looking disconnected. She told Caroline she would be out to get her after going to her office for some catch up work. Caroline noticed again how attractive Emma was. She was petite but her makeup was just perfect and every hair was in place. Emma was known around the office as being the agent who could talk anyone into anything. She had been divorced and had been in cosmetic sales before Real Estate. Maybe that was why she knew how to put makeup on so skillfully. Today she seemed pre occupied with something other than Real Estate.

Finally after about an hour Emma paged Caroline to come to her office. Caroline grabbed her notebook and hurried in. Emma's office was not as fancy as Patricia's, however, it was comfortable. You could tell Emma was not as organized as Patricia. Emma let Caroline know what she expected them to do for the next two weeks. Her demands were less stringent than Patricia's and offered in a more pleasant way. Emma surprised Caroline by saying, "I hope what happened at my listing won't affect our working together. I respect my bosses and if they feel you are worth the time to train I will gladly do my best." "Oh, no, I have almost forgotten that happened. I apologize if I should have called you before showing the house. The people bought it so if the clients were okay I plan to forget it ever happened. They are my first priority," Caroline said.

"Good I am glad. So I would like to start today with just going over what appointments we have for the week. It will be very busy. I want you to go everywhere I go this week so you can get an idea of everything that needs done from start to finish," Emma answered. She was just so much gentler in her comments than Patricia had been. Caroline really might enjoy her time with Emma after all.

Upon arriving home a few evenings later, Caroline had a letter from Bill. It had the usual things about how he would love to see her and missed home very much. Apparently without saying as much it was very bad where he was and it was taking its toll on him. At the end of the letter was a real surprise. Bill said he understood that Caroline was worried about the cost of Australia and his company was offered a chance to come home a month early if they would forfeit their trip for R&R. He really would like to come home early but he also wanted to see her soon. He continued to write that he would let her decide. Oh, great, now another decision. Caroline had thought she had everything figured out and now another boomer rang into the mix. She laid the letter down and threw herself across the bed. She didn't even care that she had on her good clothes and her mascara was running everywhere. It had been a hard week and she was just exhausted from work and her brain just couldn't take any more thinking. She would make her decision soon because she could not let this get in the way of her loving her job but missing Bill. It seemed like forever since they were together. Bill and Caroline had known each other for such a short time it almost seemed they had been apart more than they were together. Sometimes trying to imagine what he looked like would have been hard if she didn't have his picture sitting on her dresser to remind her.

It was really hard for Caroline to work the next day. She even started cleaning some of her drawers out even though they didn't need it. Keeping busy for her was an essential act of preservation. Caroline received a call from Nancy, her old school friend, and she wanted to meet for lunch that afternoon. Caroline was relieved to know she could talk to someone who would know what she should do and help her. It had been forever since they had seen each. It was really terrible that Caroline had let her job take over her life so much. She missed her friends. They agreed to meet at place they used to go to all the time when they were in school.

Caroline could hardly wait to catch up with Nancy about things that had happened to both. She didn't even know who Nancy went to sell Real Estate with. Walking back into a place Caroline used to enjoy coming and spending time with her friends brought back so many memories. She looked for Nancy for a few minutes and finally saw her sitting in the back and it seemed she had changed her looks so much. Nancy always had a smile on her face and she was not real pretty but kept herself immaculate. Walking towards her Caroline hardly recognized her. She had cut her hair really short and looked 10 years older. They hugged before Caroline sat down. "How have you been? I am so sorry we haven't kept in touch but between training and working I haven't had much time for anything," Caroline said. Nancy stared at her for a minute and then proceeded to tell Caroline why she had wanted to see her. "I feel bad too but I have had other things going on. I never got a chance to start my Real Estate career. My husband needed me so much after he returned home that I felt I had to take care of him. It was so hard for him to be left alone because of his PTSD. The medication he was on really did nothing but make him sleep all the time," Nancy replied very quietly. Caroline was shocked since Nancy was such a go getter in school. "I am so sorry to hear your husband is not doing better. I was hoping his rehab would get him back home and doing well. Is there anything I can do for you?" Nancy looked up at Caroline and started to cry, "I am afraid there is nothing anyone can do now. He overdosed over the weekend and passed away at the hospital the next day. I can't tell you how hard it has been. That damn war is going to destroy all of us if we aren't careful." Caroline could hardly believe what she was hearing. What kind of friend had she been not to keep in touch and be there for Nancy when she needed her so much? Here Caroline was worrying about her little problems and Nancy had lost her husband. There is no way I can ask her what I should do now. They proceeded to place their orders. Nancy, of course, ordered very little. You could tell looking at her she had not been eating and it was so sad to see her in the shape she was. They talked for awhile and Caroline ask her again if she could do anything.

"No if you would just have lunch with me once in awhile so I can keep my mind busy. I really do want to start working so I can stay busy. How is your new boss and do you think they would hire me if I came to work there?" Nancy said. Caroline almost felt she was blushing before saying, "It is a great place and I really don't feel it is really work at all. It is so much fun and I have learned so much from other agents. I even sold my first listing the other day!" Caroline proceeded to fill Nancy in on other things when she asked Nancy ask how Bill was and Caroline wanted to go into it but felt it just wasn't a good time. They finished lunch and agreed to meet again next week same time and place. All the way back to work all Caroline could think about was how awful this place Bill was at had to be. She had felt from Bills letters it was bad but hearing Nancy's story just confirmed it. Caroline had avoided watching the news because it seemed like that Vietnam was all that was on. How many were killed and hurt each day. She immediately made up her mind right then that she had to see Bill and not wait. As soon as she arrived home that evening she wrote him that she would really like to see him sooner rather than later.

Caroline spent the next week talking to a travel agent about booking her reservations and trying to make sure she really knew what this was going to cost. It made it very exciting planning a trip like this. She had heard Australia was beautiful and she had never been anywhere outside the states before. After she had everything pretty well planned she sent Bill all the info and told him how excited she was about the trip. He almost always was able to write in a week's time unless he was out in the field so she waited anxiously for his reply. She was a little worried he would rather have come home early but she hoped this trip would be something they both could look forward to.

Emma was keeping Caroline busy with appointments and open houses. She seemed to let Caroline do as much work as she could and she would just answer any questions and look over all the paperwork. It was starting to be easier now that Caroline had been working for awhile and learning from experienced agents. She knew now that Derek really had known what he was doing setting her up with these agents. Of course, she found everyone at the office that she had gotten to know had their own little quirks but most of them were really nice people and it really felt like a family instead of work. She could not imagine who he would have her working with next. She still had not decided whether to tell Derek about Emma's little escapade in the hot tub. Emma had really been so nice to her that Caroline hated to say anything but she also knew Derek should know in case it happened again.

Caroline was working at her desk one morning and she received a message across the PA system that she had a call on line two. As she looked down at her phone she noticed the call was from Bill's mom. It was a shock in a way because she had stayed in touch with Bill's family but not daily or even weekly. She had been so busy and it just didn't seem to be something she thought about. Picking up the phone Caroline answered almost like a question. "Hi, Ann, how are you today? I hope everything is okay." There was a long pause and Caroline had thought maybe she had gotten disconnected but then Bill's mom said, "Caroline I don't know how to tell you this but we just received a telegram from Bills commander that he is missing in action." Caroline almost dropped the phone. She didn't know what to say it was such a shock. She had just gotten a letter from him not that long ago. "Oh, my god Ann. I don't know what to say. I just heard from Bill and he seemed down but I hadn't heard people were going missing in action that much. I had assumed the worst that could happen was him being wounded," Caroline replied in sort of a whimper. Bill's mom told her they were waiting for more info from the Defense Department. It could just be he had gotten lost in the jungle or injured and still might be fine. She told Caroline she would stay in touch if she heard anything.

Caroline sat at her desk for a long time staring into space. Not knowing how to react. This was something that happened to other people, not her. There was no way she could work anymore today so she ask Emma for the rest of the day off for personal business. Caroline went straight home and crawled into bed. It was like she was struck by lightning. Crying came easy but you could only cry so much and then what. That did not answer any questions about what had happened. Caroline decided it would be better to be busy so she decided to call Nancy and see if she could meet her over coffee and answer the many questions inside her head. Her husband had been in Vietnam and she might know other people who were missing in action.

Nancy seemed almost glad to meet with Caroline at the diner they always went. Sitting down across from Nancy, it seemed to Caroline that her friend was doing better. Her color was back and she seemed in a better spirit. "What do you want to talk about? I was so glad you called. I have been going through things of my husbands and I needed a break," Nancy said. "Well, I hope I don't upset you but Bill has been reported Missing In Action and I am about to go crazy wondering exactly what this means as far as if it is possible he might be alright or do I just accept the fact that he is never coming back?", Caroline replied almost in tears. Nancy was shocked at first and then it seemed she did not want to show her fear to Caroline so she began by saying, "It doesn't always mean the worst. His unit might have just gone out on patrol and have not returned in the time period that is expected. If they sent a telegram it is more alarming because he has probably been missing for a few days."

Caroline was somewhat relieved but not totally at ease and said, "I think I know but what is the worst thing that has happened? Is it possible he has been captured? All these things keep running through my head." Nancy tried to reassure Caroline and to try to assume the best if she could. She told her to try to stay busy and if Bills parents could they might try to reach Bill's commander or someone in charge since Caroline probably would not be allowed to since she was not yet his wife. They talked a little while longer. Caroline did not want to wake up bad memories for Nancy.

As soon as Caroline returned home she contacted Bill's mom to see how they were doing. She asked if they had received any more info and passed along what Nancy had suggested about trying to reach someone in command who might be able to answer questions. Bill's mom was upset naturally, however, she was a very brave woman. She had already lost a daughter to an illness at a young age and she seemed a little numb to things compared to other people. Bill had always felt his Mom had lost part of herself when his sister died. After they hung up, Caroline felt sure that they would try to find something out. It would be so hard returning to work but she needed to stay busy.

Before she got ready for bed her phone rang. It was Derek wanting to know if she was okay. He knew she wouldn't miss work unless it was something serious. Caroline, trying to sound okay, said, "It's Bill he has gone Missing In Action. I just feel like I have let him down. I haven't been staying in touch like I should and he knew I hesitated when it came to R&R. I don't even know if he received my letter telling him I was coming after all." Derek was quiet so long Caroline was not sure he was on the other end but finally he said, "Oh, Caroline I am so sorry. You shouldn't blame yourself for anything that has happened. He will be alright since he has you to come back to." Wow that almost sounded like Derek was jealous that Bill had her to come back to, but he was probably just trying to make her feel better. They talked for awhile and Caroline told Derek she wanted to stay busy so she would be back in to work tomorrow. It had made Caroline feel better to know she had friends that she could confide in and her own parents who were equally upset since they really liked Bill from the first time they met him.

Time went by slowly but Caroline was finishing up her work with Emma and decided she had made a friend for life. Emma was so ordinary yet very smart. She could teach Caroline a lot about the business. Every Tuesday there was a staff meeting and it was an all day event looking at new listings and getting a chance to share with other agents. Derek went on these tours which was unusual since most Managing Brokers did not join their agents. It seemed it made him closer to everyone and he even took turns riding with different agents. Caroline had gotten a chance to ride with him this Tuesday and it was the most fun she had in a long time. They went to one house and could not get in. It turned out they were at the wrong house since the numbers were turned around on the showing sheet. It was embarrassing but thank goodness the owners were not home. At another house a dog wanted in so they let it in and come to find out it was not the owner's dog. The owner called to say the dog was a neighbors and always wanted in her house. She said she came home right away and everything was okay. There was always something happening and you just had to laugh about it. Staying busy was helpful but Caroline still could not help but worry.

After two weeks she received a letter in the mail. After figuring out who sent it she was both relieved and upset. Things were only getting worse and her life was about to change forever.

Chapter 12

The letter was lying on Caroline's dressing table when she arrived home. Her mom always placed her mail there so she would be sure and see it. It looked like it had been in someone's pocket for a long time. Wrinkled and stained it was almost like it had been thrown away and then retrieved. Caroline could not tell who sent it since there was no return address. She opened it slowly almost like she was expecting to explode in her hands. The paper inside appeared to be just an old scrap of paper that appeared to be as a last resort for something to write on. As she read she was shocked and relieved at the same time.

Dearest Caroline,

I am sorry to have to write you this letter but I just had to explain my actions.

I am doing okay even though it has been a hectic last few days. Another soldier and I decided we had to leave Vietnam or we would leave only in body bags. This friend of mine had friends in the transport of equipment and supplies and we were able to hide aboard a plane that was headed to the Philippines. He was able to have passports created with fake ids and we are on our way to Canada on the next plane out.

I know this has to be hard for you but in my mental state I would not be much use to you for awhile anyway. When I get settled in Canada I will contact you and we can talk about you joining me there. The worst thing is I can never return to the United States unless later on the government decides to give amnesty to everyone who left. There are many of us so I highly doubt that will happen.

I love you and wanted to spend the rest of my life with you, however, I am not of much use to anyone right now even myself.

With Love,
Bill

Caroline laid the letter down and began to cry. It seems the part of her life with Bill had just ended as soon as she read this letter. After talking with her friend Nancy she was not surprised by this happening but Bill had always been such a strong person she never would have thought he would run away from his responsibility unless it was really a desperate move.

Thank goodness it was Friday and Caroline would have the weekend to think about what was happening to her life. She immediately called Nancy to let her know what had happened to see if she could help Caroline see the whole picture of why someone would do this. Nancy agreed to meet her at their favorite place and they talked for a long time about Bills motives. Nancy made Caroline realize how bad their existence was in Vietnam and the danger everyday of being sent home but not the same person that left. After their conversation Caroline realized if she really cared for Bill she would just be glad he left when he did and hope in future to be able to see him again. Caroline cancelled her plans for the trip they had planned together and tried to decide what to do next with her life. Could she wait for a long time to get her life on to the next stage? It was very depressing to think there was no end in sight to the waiting for the person she was going to marry to be able to begin a life with her.

It was hard but Caroline returned to work that Monday. She needed to talk to Derek and see who she was supposed to work with for the next few weeks. Emma had been a great teacher and they really enjoyed each other's company. She felt she still would have to tell Derek the incident at the showing where Emma had been naked but she was trying to think of a way to make it seem innocent and that was going to hard to do.

Derek's secretary said he was in and so Caroline knocked on his door. He told her to come in and seemed pleased that it was her. "I just wanted to see if you had someone in mind for me to work with these next few weeks?" she said.

"I really feel you have learned quite a bit and unless you feel like you need it I am going to give you a few weeks just to see how you can do on your own. I know you have been working really hard and probably need a chance to catch up on your paperwork and personal things. Have you heard anything new about Bill being missing?" Derek said.

She wasn't sure how to tell him that Bill wasn't coming back. It made Bill seem like a bad person but she hoped everyone including Derek would understand and not judge him for what he had done.

"Bill isn't missing in action. He has runaway to Canada to avoid having to spend any more time in Vietnam. It became so bad he said he could not take it any longer. I received a letter from him letting me know over the weekend. I guess I am going to have to change all my plans for the future. It will take time but I am hoping with your help here at the office and my friends I can try to get on with my life, "Caroline said looking down almost ashamed.

"Oh, my gosh, how awful for you. Is there anything I can do to help you get through this? I can't imagine what you are going through. Don't ever feel like you are alone as long as I am a part of your life," Derek replied with a pleading sound to his voice.

"You are so nice to me. I can't tell you how much it means to me to know you understand what I am going through. Bill and I had grown close for such a short time it has almost became a distant past and the present seems more real and necessary. I will try to do everything to make you proud of me as an employee and also to try not to be too needy," Caroline said almost in a whisper.

Derek and Caroline finished talking about the report she needed to write about her work with Emma. Derek proceeded to tell Caroline he was going to the Indianapolis office next weekend and wanted to know if she would like to get away and see some of the great places in Indy. She thought about it about a second and told him she would love get away and learn more about the office in Indianapolis. She had already had to do business with the Relocation department there and wanted to get to know them more in person.

Later on in the week when she thought more about the conversation she thought maybe she sounded too anxious. Anything sounded good as long as it was to stay busy and not have to think about what was going to happen when Bill contacted her again and wanted her to come to Canada. She already knew the answer to that.

Chapter 13

The weekend came around very quickly and Caroline was looking forward to getting away. Derek offered to pick her up early Saturday morning. The road to Indianapolis from Southern Indiana was a beautiful trip this time of year. It ended up the forecast was for great weather all weekend. Caroline was a little nervous since she had not been alone in a car with Derek and she was afraid she would talk too much as she usually did when she was nervous. They rode for awhile in silence and then Derek initiated the conversation by saying he was glad Caroline had decided to join him. "I didn't want you to think I was being too pushy by asking you to join me this weekend but I thought you needed some time away. You know I have tried to give you plenty of space for when you decide what your plans are with Bill will be but I would like the opportunity to spend more time with you on your terms," Derek said with his eyes on the road.

"I am glad you suggested this. I promise that I just can't spend my whole life planning a future that might not ever happen. I love working with everyone and my job is even more wonderful than I thought it would be. Being with you is always so comfortable and I don't see why we can't spend time working and enjoying time together. You are a friend just like lots of other people in my life," Caroline said thinking afterward that it sounded very platonic.

It had gotten really quiet so Caroline enjoyed the scenery and waited for Derek to say something else. He seemed almost hurt by her answer but maybe she was just imagining it.

They finally reached the hotel and Derek checked them in since he had made the reservations. Caroline just assumed they would have separate rooms but she almost thought about what it would be like if they shared a room instead. My gosh, she thought to herself, what is wrong with you? You need to get hold of yourself and remember you still have someone else counting on you to make some kind of commitment.

They went to their rooms together and her room ended up being right next to Derek's. She was both relieved and disappointed. He told her he would let her get settled and then they could go to the office where he could get some things done he needed to do. Caroline unpacked her things and freshened up. This room wasn't as nice as the first she had stayed in but it was very nice and it was apparently formerly one big area made to adjoin another room. She could hear Derek talking on the phone on the other side of the door but did not actually think anything about it since they often made one room two on busy weekends in hotels. In a few minutes Derek called to say he would be right over and they would just walk to the office since it adjoined the hotel.

Caroline found plenty to do while Derek was getting whatever work he needed to do. She met with some of the agents at that office and got a chance to find out where everything was located in case she needed anything. When Derek was done they decided to go get something to eat since both of them were famished. He always seemed to know what she was thinking almost before she did.

They went to a favorite restaurant of the locals. Very informal but the food was excellent. It was dark and they found a booth in the back that was away from the noise of the music that was filtered in. It was hard to sit too far apart since it was one of those U shaped booths that faced forward only. It didn't bother Caroline at all since she had gotten real comfortable with Derek and he was always such a gentleman.

After they ordered and were waiting for their food Derek started the conversation with a surprising sentence, "Do you know what you are going to do about going to Canada? We would hate to lose a good agent. Especially since you seem to have really caught on fast and one of the most professional agents I have seen in a long time."

Caroline hesitated hoping it was more than about her being a good agent. "I promise you will be the one of the first to know when I decide. I realize you have plenty of people who would love to work at your company and I would not want you to lose out because I stayed too long. I will not spend the rest of my life waiting for Bill. According to my good friend Nancy life with someone returning from Vietnam is more than likely a future with many problems. I feel bad since Bill did not choose to go but I feel we did not have enough time together before he left to really get to know each other."

Derek seemed pleased with her answer and then toasted Caroline to hoping her decision would be an easy one. They ate and had some small talk but otherwise just enjoyed their wonderful meal together. There was a dance floor and Derek asks Caroline if she would like to dance. It had been so long since she had danced with anyone she was almost afraid to try but she had just enough wine to give her courage.

The song playing was one of her favorite, Can't Take My Eyes Off Of You, by Frankie Vallie. Derek seemed to be very careful how he held Caroline so not to make her feel obligated to be too close. As the song played Caroline really enjoyed the dance. Having Derek so near for the first time she made the mistake of looking into those blue eyes and it was unlike anything she had ever felt. From her head to her toes she tingled. It scared her in a way since she felt bad enjoying herself so much with Bill gone but somehow she had to start caring about her feelings for a change. Caroline could tell Derek was enjoying the dance as much as she was. When she looked into his eyes he did not look away but continued to look into her eyes and he smiled like he was glad she was enjoying the dance. They had a couple more glasses of wine and decided to go back to the room. Derek had said his work was done and they could go sightseeing or shopping whatever she wanted to do before they headed home.

Derek walked Caroline to her door and gave her a peck on the cheek. Kind of disappointing but Caroline really respected Derek for being so thoughtful about her situation. Caroline decided to call home and get to work writing her report for Derek about Emma. She had put it off so long and she wanted to get it over with. In the report she let Derek know what happened in the hot tub at the listing but inferred since that time she had seen nothing that would cause the company concern.

Caroline walked past the connecting door to get to the bathroom and heard Derek talking to someone. She assumed he was on the phone and did not think anything about it. Coming out of the shower and back into the room Caroline noticed Derek was talking louder and a woman's voice was a very high pitch for normal conversation. She did not want to eavesdrop but she couldn't help it. The voice coming from his room sounded like Emma's but surely that would be ridiculous since she would not be in Indianapolis. Caroline listened for the voices to stop and decided to pretend she was delivering her report just so she could find out what was going on. As she put her clothes back on, since she had changed into her night clothes, Caroline proceeded to open her door to the hall and as she did Emma was walking into the elevator but did not see Caroline. When Caroline knew Emma was gone she knocked on Derek's door. He answered almost right away and appeared to be out of breath and upset about something. Caroline was afraid he was mad at her for bothering him.

"I am sorry but I thought I had better bring you this report about Emma that I forgot to give to you before we left home. I tried to be very honest but understanding of the one thing I felt was a problem. If you want to read it and give me a call when you get a chance I can answer any of your questions, "said in a hurry hoping to be on her way.

"Oh, Caroline, I am sorry. I hope we weren't too loud awhile ago. I do need to explain something to you anyway. I was going to call you in a little while. The reason I came to Indianapolis was to have a meeting with my Dad and some of the other owners of the company. Let me read your letter. Have a glass a wine while I am reading or anything else on the room service tray, "Derek said almost relieved sounding.

Caroline decided she had too much wine already but poured herself a glass of water. She watched Derek read the letter and he was almost smiling as he got to the part about the hot tub. He finished reading the letter and as he laid it down he looked up at her and said, "This certainly makes my explanation for her being here easier to explain to you. Emma was the one in the basement that night you were scared. She was with a client and they were in a very compromising position. This was not the first time that had happened. I ask that she see a phyciatrist if she wanted to continue to work for us. Evidently she has a nymphomaniac problem and I cannot allow it to interfere with our business. I came here today to ask her to either come to the Indy office or see a doctor here or she would be fired. She is a valuable asset to our company financially but we cannot have someone with a problem like that and having things happen like the hot tub problem. It makes our company look really bad. I am sorry you had to work with her but I knew you would be professional about it and keep it to yourself. Emma was one of the reasons we decided to use you for spying on agents so we could make sure she was on her best behavior. I am sorry I could not tell you since you would have been looking for a problem and it might have been taken care of with her doctor's help."

Caroline was silent. It took her minute to take in what Derek was saying. All she could think about was what a nice guy to let try to help an agent instead of firing her the very first time. Caroline had been with Emma for two weeks and found all her other qualities to be good ones. She almost felt sorry for her. "I can't believe the beautiful, successful woman I worked for the last few weeks has a problem like that. She seemed so like all the other agents I have met except the one showing I had. I am sorry she has this problem and I hope she gets help. You are really great to be so kind to her," Caroline said.

"I hope this conversation will go no further than this room. I value Emma's privacy since it is an illness not something she can help without professional care. If she lets us down this time we will have to let her go. I really admire her ability to sell and list real estate and I feel there might be a chance she can overcome this problem. She has had a really bad past and I feel that may have something to do with her actions. The little I have heard about this disease is that women who have been treated really bad by men and gone unappreciated seem to have this problem more than others," Derek said with sadness in his voice.

Caroline decided it was time to return to the room since they both were tired. It was going to be a hard night to try and sleep with all the things going through her head. The things with Emma but also the way she felt while they were dancing. Just thinking about it made a chill go up her spine like nothing before. Just thinking about their time together was so special and made her feel alive like she hadn't for a long time.

The next day they visited the sights of Indy and went shopping at places like Caroline had never shopped. She had been a small southern Indiana girl her whole life and never went anywhere since they were so poor. Of course, she didn't want to act too excited

Chapter 14

Returning home from Indianapolis was uneventful. Both Derek and Caroline were very quiet. Each one was thinking about what had developed over the weekend. Derek was thinking about how Caroline seemed more receptive to his closeness and Caroline was thinking about Emma's situation and what it would be like knowing that about her. The good thing was that Emma would be working in another office and that would certainly make it easier.

Upon returning back to work Monday Caroline decided to put her thoughts in making sure she was the best agent she could be. The secret she had found was working lots of hours and making Real Estate your life and not your profession. She had looked at all the successful agents in her office and it seemed they spent all their time working or socializing for work. Caroline certainly would have the time to do that now.

Weeks started turning into months and Caroline had still not heard from Bill. She tried not to think about it but it was hard not to. She wanted to get on with her life if he was not going to want to continue their relationship but she also did not want to make him feel any worse about his decision to go to Canada. She had been reading a lot about soldiers that had left for Canada so it was not all that unusual. Some were in the worst part of the war and they were hit the hardest with their friends being killed in the trench right next to them or blown up in front of them when someone stepped on a land mine. It was not always the enemy's land mines either. It was ours sometimes which made it even worse. The first guy to step on it was always killed and it was not something the others could forget easily.

Caroline had decided to see Derek through business meetings and lunches but Derek had really been nice about not pressuring her to go our socially. She had told him she would have to finish one part of her life before she could even start another. That was getting to be hard on her and she was afraid Derek would move on. She encouraged him to see other people but really she did not want him to in fear he would fall in love with someone.

Sometime close to Carolinas one year anniversary with the company Derek ask if she would meet with him in his office. She wondered if she had done something wrong. He very seldom asks for private meetings with her unless it was business related. He was sitting at his desk talking on the phone so he gestured for her to sit down. It wasn't long before he hung up the phone and he wrote some information down before starting the conversation. "I hope you don't get upset about what I have done. I just couldn't watch you waiting any longer to hear from Bill. I hired a private detective to try to find where Bill is at in Canada. I made sure no one else would find out the information since it might cause problems for you and Bill. I just got off the phone with the private detective and he has found an address for Bill. He is living at a homeless shelter and working during the day."

Caroline sat stunned for a minute. She was caught off guard. It had not occurred to her to do anything like that and she felt bad she didn't think of it first. "I am so relieved just to know he is okay. I was afraid he would do harm to himself. There are so many stories about that happening. The guilt of what they have done is so hard on the soldiers that run away. It seems to make them feel they are less of a man. What do I do with this information now," Caroline asks.

Derek was relieved she was not mad about what he had done. It was a selfish thing. He wanted this part of Carolinas life to be decided on. He wanted to spend more time with her and go dancing again and he knew she would not do that without knowing where her life was headed with Bill. "I thought we could fly to Canada and find Bill. I would go along just to be support and stay out of the way when you see him. You both need to talk and get some idea if your life will be together or just over for good. It wouldn't take us but a couple of days away and maybe you can move on with your life, "Derek said.

Caroline did not even hesitate. "Your right. I am tired of my life being at a standstill. If you feel we both can take the time lets go. I have never been to Canada so if nothing else it will be an adventure. If have been feeling that if he cannot at least write me then I should not be wasting my time worrying about his feelings. When do you want to leave? Caroline said excitedly.

Derek sat stunned and said, "I will make reservations for Saturday morning. I am so glad you aren't mad but I think both of us need some answers. I will pick you up Saturday morning."

The flight was really wonderful. The scenery from the sky was amazing. Caroline couldn't believe how many times she had been in a plane this last year. Her life had definitely changed from a woman waiting for her soldier to come home to a professional real estate agent making a good salary. She had learned how to dress and wear makeup. She was never a plain Jane but compared to now she certainly had made a lot of good changes in her life. Even her self confidence and changed especially with the new people in her life who made her feel like she was smart and resourceful.

Derek and Caroline talked business a lot on the way; however, finally the conversation turned to what would happen in Canada. "What do you hope this trip will accomplish? Derek said. Caroline knew he would expect some kind of result after all the trouble he had gone to. She wasn't sure what she expected but she wanted to let him know she appreciated his help.

"I hope by seeing Bill I will at least feel he is going to be okay and I feel I have to let him know that I have made a life in Indiana that I really don't want to give up. It will be hard to tell him that but I have to be honest with him," Caroline replied.

Derek let her know he hoped she would find out what she needed and she could return home with a better feeling about her life. They enjoyed the flight without much more talk the rest of the trip to Canada.

Chapter 15

Caroline had always heard Canada was very beautiful but she had no idea how much green landscape and white capped mountains there were. She just expected cold. Of course, it was summer so it was the perfect weather since it never reached high humidity like Indiana did.

After they checked into their hotel Caroline wanted to go immediately to the address the private detective had given Derek. They rented a car with a GPS and Derek proceeded to drive her to the homeless shelter. It was fairly easy to find since it was located in mid-town. It was a fairly run down building and you could tell the neighborhood was not the best. Derek decided to wait while Caroline went in just to keep from causing any kind of problems for her.

Caroline went to the front desk where there was a scraggly bearded older man who was half asleep but woke up when she cleared her throat. "I am looking for someone named Bill. Could you tell me if he is living here?"

"Well madam there are lots of Bill's around here. Would you happen to have a last name?" he said.

She felt really stupid. Of course, there was more than one Bill. How could she be so dumb?

"Kincaid is his last name." She happened to think he might have changed it since the guy behind the counter had a strange look on his face. "Tall and thin," she told him trying to picture him. It had been so long since she had seen him she had to try and think about it more than she would have liked to.

"You family? He left a letter if someone showed up. He said she would be pretty if it was a young lady but he didn't describe you as beautiful," the old man winked as he said it. "Let me get it. I put it away so it wouldn't get lost. Just a minute."

A letter! Why would he leave a letter not knowing she would come or not. That was strange. He brought it out to her. It looked a lot like the other letter she received from him. Wrinkled and torn but still readable. It had her name on the outside so she knew it was for her. For a minute she stood there and then ask again if he lived there. The old man at the desk said "Just read the letter is what he told me to tell you."

Caroline went back out to the car that Derek was patiently waiting in. He asks her when she got in the car why she was back so soon. "He left me a letter. They wouldn't tell me if he lived there or not. Just told me to read the letter, so I guess if you don't mind lets go get a drink before I open this. I am not sure it can be a great letter from the feeling I got inside that awful place."

They drove for awhile until they found a small café that looked welcoming and quaint. Caroline headed for the back of the restaurant to a booth that was all to itself so they could have some privacy. Derek ordered them something to drink and Caroline proceeded to open the letter.

Dear Caroline,

I left this letter just in case it was you that had someone looking for me. I heard from the front desk that there was a private investigator that was looking for me. They said they did not tell him I was here definitely but I was sure if it was you that somehow you would come. I pretty much knew it was not my parents as they would not have the extra money to look for me.

I am sorry that I did not get to see you but I thought it was best. I have just found a job and moved from the shelter. I still look have so many problems and would not want you to see me like I am. At first I took drugs to ease the memories but then I found a friend who helped me go to rehab and so far I have been clean for 6 months. They helped me get a fairly good job. I had some training in the service so it seems that helped me get the job.

I don't want you to think I don't love you anymore but I just had to let you get on with your life. I am such a mess I would not want children and that was something you said was important to you. Please forget about me, however, if I can ever return to the states I will let you know and see if we can still be friends.

Good luck with your life and please know that this is the best thing for both of us.

Love Always,
Bill

As Caroline was reading the letter tears were running down her cheeks. She was heartbroken that their life together was over. She knew Bill was right. Their future would be awful. She knew from what Nancy had gone through with her husband that it could take years for Bill to ever be the same if ever.

Derek could tell something about the letter was very upsetting to Caroline but he wanted her to have time to comprehend it and patiently waited for her to tell him its contents. He kept wondering if it would mean she could be his after all or was that being selfish not to want her to be happy.

Caroline stared at the letter for quite awhile like it wasn't really there. She had to tell Derek what it said but was afraid she would start crying again and wouldn't be able to finish. "Bill has asked that I forget about him and go on with my life. He says he is unfit for a normal life now and maybe in the future. He says he never wants children and knows how important that is to me. I don't know whether to feel glad he has been honest with me because it hurts so badly but it means that the wondering is over. It is going to be hard but I have to start forgetting about the past and move on to the future," she said not wanting to sound harsh.

"I am so sorry. I know your heart must be breaking. You loved this man and he no longer is the same man you fell in love with. That has to be so hard. Let's go back to the hotel and we can head home on a plane in the morning unless you need more time here," Derek said with sympathy in his voice.

They went back to the hotel and Caroline ask Derek if she could have some time to think before dinner that evening. He, of course, felt she needed that time to think some more if she needed to.

What was really crazy was Caroline did not want to cry. She was almost relieved that she would not have to worry anymore about keeping her promises to Bill. They had known each other such a short time and Caroline did not realize what it truly felt like to feel the electricity she felt when she was around Derek. She had grown much attached to him and the attraction she felt for him was overwhelming. She had to think how she would proceed without seeming to thoughtless about what Bill had been through. Yes she had loved him but not like you should love someone you would spend the rest of your life with. She decided she would tell Derek this evening at dinner what she was feeling.

They decided to eat at one of the restaurants in the mountains that were recommended by a hotel guest. It took them awhile to get there but the road was full of beautiful scenery so it seemed closer than it was. They arrived to a restaurant that was built into a mountain almost like it was being swallowed by the overhangs and there was still now on the mountains in Canada. All the way there

Caroline thought about what she would say to Derek. She did not have to worry about that after all. It seems Derek had being doing some of his own thinking. As they were seated, a waiter brought them the best wine in the house. Caroline just knew it was very expensive because she had wanted to order it before and decided it was too expensive. After they ordered their food Derek decided he wanted to toast Caroline for hopefully being able to go on with her life. He seemed happy that she might be able to at least give him some more attention now that her old life was behind her.

"I don't want to seem presumptuous but I hope you will let me know when I can really start letting you know how I feel. I think you know but I wasn't sure you knew how much," Derek said as he raised his glass. Caroline was relieved that he felt the way she thought he did. She blushed from the attention he was paying her and enjoying every minute of it.

"I know it seems wrong for me to seem so fickle but I have wanted to be with you more but somehow felt guilty before. Of course, I know we both have a lot of things to consider as we proceed but I am looking forward to seeing more of you and I don't mean at work. It seems that's the only time I get to be with you and we need to really get to know other things about each other. You might decide I am not who you want to be with," Caroline said as she raised her glass to him.

As their glasses met and they looked into each other's eyes they knew this was going to be a wonderful adventure. She loved her new career and especially her new boss.

Caroline went to work at one of their branches in town. Derek didn't think it was a good idea or professional to be dating an agent at his own office. They still could see each other at meetings and house tours. Of course, every weekend they weren't working they were looking for house for their selves and that big family that they planned in a few years after Caroline got selling houses out of her blood. That might not ever happen but it makes a nice profession for mothers with grown children also.

Their wedding was planned for that next summer. Caroline waited awhile just to be sure it was true love this time and she was sure even a war would not come between her and the man she loved this time. No matter what!

Printed in the United States
By Bookmasters